The Secret Horse

The Secret Horse

by MARION HOLLAND

Illustrated by Taylor Oughton

SCHOLASTIC INC.
NEW YORK · TORONTO · LONDON · AUCKLAND · SYDNEY · TOKYO

For my three daughters,
Barbara and Judith and Rebecca.
They know why.

ISBN 0-590-03845-1

16 15 14 13 12 11 10 9 8 7 6 4 5 6 7/8

Printed in the U.S.A. 01

Contents

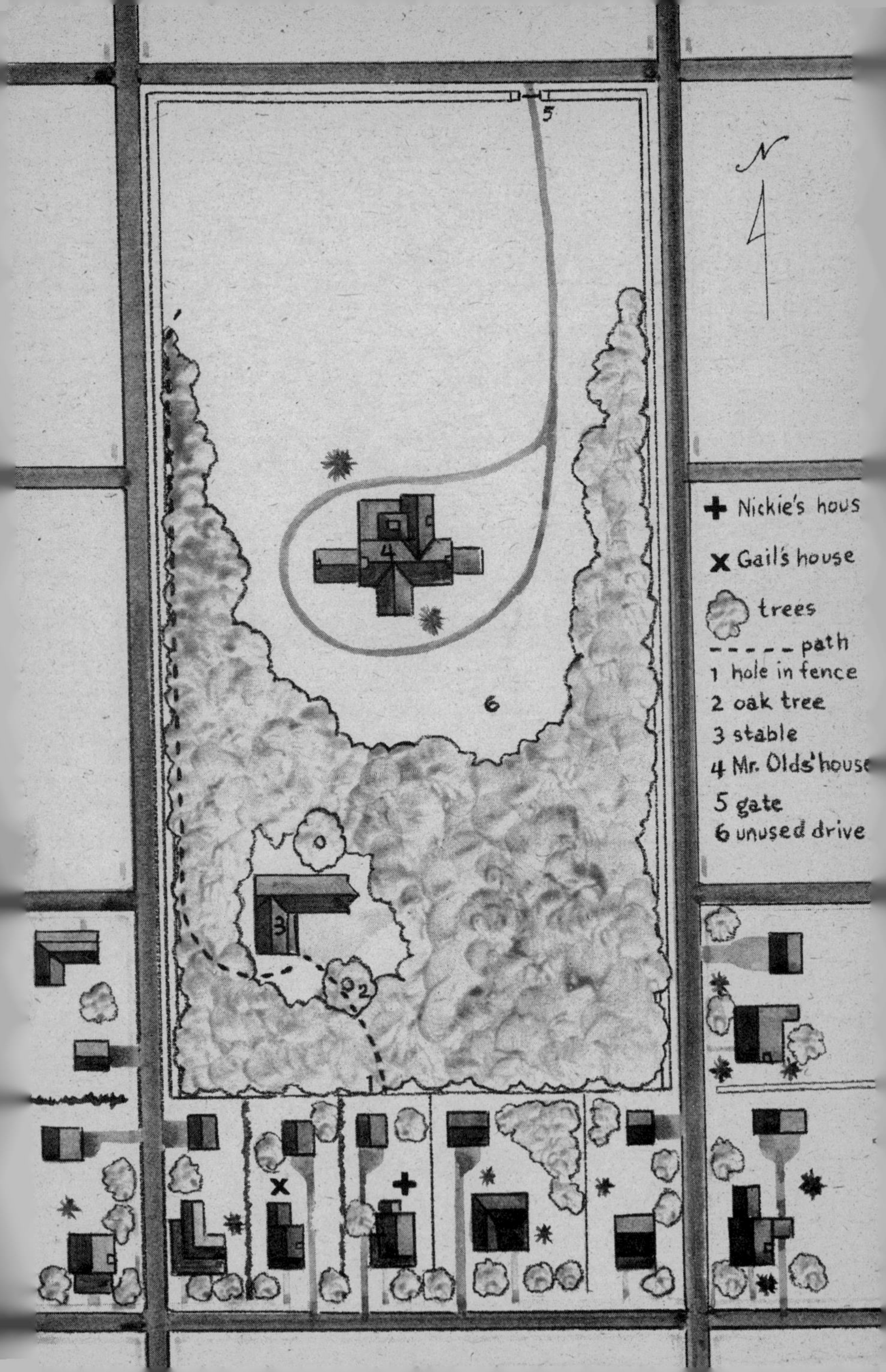

N
Nickie's hous
Gail's house
trees
path
1 hole in fence
2 oak tree
3 stable
4 Mr. Olds' house
5 gate
6 unused drive
1
2
3
4
5
6

The 27th of June

Nickie Baxter looked up from her cornflakes and asked suddenly, "Does anybody happen to know what day it is today?"

"Why, no, dear. What day is it?" asked her mother, dropping two more pieces of bread in the toaster.

"Thursday, the twenty-sixth," said Nickie's brother, Roger. "Or is it the twenty-seventh? ... Marmalade, please."

Nickie's father looked up from the morning paper. "Today is the twenty-seventh of June," he said. "Why? Is there something special about it?"

"Oh, no, nothing special about it," replied Nickie, letting a spoonful of cornflakes dribble back into the bowl. "Nothing special at all," she said resentfully. "Just that it happens to be the first day of camp. Just that today everybody will be rushing up to their tents and dumping their suitcases on their bunks and then rushing down to the stables to see if all the horses are back. Everybody, that is, except me. I can't see why — "

"Nickie, dear, you can see why," interrupted her mother patiently. "We've been over it all a hundred times."

"A thousand times," mumbled Roger.

"We simply cannot afford it this year," her mother continued. "We had to have a whole new front porch on account of the termites. And new beams under the living room as well."

"Why did we have to? *Why*?" demanded Nickie. I'm going to be stuck here all summer while all my friends are away at camp. And I'll probably never even *see* a horse until next summer."

Mr. Baxter lowered his newspaper and looked across the table at his daughter's stormy face. "Nickie, we aren't going to listen to this all summer. We all know that you were counting on camp, and we're sorry. Now stop mooning about it and find something to do. Find somebody to play with."

"Who? Tell me who? Joan's already at camp. Mollie's sewing on name tapes like crazy because she goes tomorrow, and Debby left last week for her uncle's farm in Indiana. And he raises trotting horses too! Oh, I wish we could sell this awful old house and buy a farm so I could have a horse. I'm just the unluckiest girl in the whole world!"

"*Annick*!" roared Mr. Baxter.

Her father hardly ever called her Annick, and when he did, he meant business. Nickie lowered her eyes to her cereal bowl and stirred the cornflakes around in little circles.

Mr. Baxter looked at his watch and stood up. He folded the paper, picked up his briefcase, and kissed his wife good-bye. At the doorway he stopped and looked back at Nickie's dark, curly head, still bent over the cereal bowl.

"Nickie," he said gently, "you're not unlucky. You're a very lucky little girl and you're old enough to think about it. You're healthy and pretty and you have a family that loves you. You have a nice place to live and you have plenty to eat and to wear. I'm sorry about the horse, but you could get a puppy or a kitten to take care of as long as you'll be home all summer. Now I must run or I'll be late."

The front door banged and Mr. Baxter sprinted down the steps to catch the bus to his office in Washington.

Nickie's mother said cheerfully, "Eat your cornflakes, dear, before they get all soggy."

"They're soggy already," mumbled Nickie. "I don't want them. I don't want a puppy or a kitten either. I want a horse."

"But you must eat something," urged her mother.

"Why?" Roger asked, piling marmalade on the last piece of toast. "If she starves to death, she'll be out of her misery."

His mother shook her head at him. "Cheer up, Nickie. Mrs. Walton told me last week that her son and his wife will be staying with her for a while. They came last night and they have two children. One is a girl just your age. Isn't that nice?"

"I guess so," muttered Nickie.

"I'm sure you'll like each other. They were here years ago — when you were about three. I remember you went to the little girl's birthday party."

"I don't remember," said Nickie.

"I do," said Roger emphatically. "You took a present to her party and when you got there you wouldn't give it to her. When the party was over, you brought it home again. I had to take it back and give it to the kid."

"I did not. Did I, Mother?"

"I don't remember, dear, and I'm sure she won't remember either. Now run upstairs and tidy your room. Roger, your father hopes to find some paint on the porch when he gets home this evening."

As Nickie started for the back stairs, Roger called after her, "Hey, small fry! Who won the Kentucky Derby in 1948?"

It was an old game they played, but Nickie didn't feel like playing it this morning.

"Citation," she said sulkily.

"Well, go on. Your turn."

"Who won the World Series in 1955? As if I cared."

"The Brooklyn Dodgers!" shouted Roger as he clattered down to the basement for the paint and brushes.

The Girl Next Door

Nickie dragged herself up the back stairs to her room and shut the door. Her rumpled bed was under the sunny back window.

Her pajamas lay in the middle of the floor, right where she had gotten out of them. On the desk there was a calendar, with a picture of a horse on it and a big red circle around the 27th of June.

"I hate everybody," Nickie mumbled as she kicked her pajamas through the open closet door and slammed it shut.

She went over to her bed and jerked the sheet and bedspread up over the dented pillow. The bed looked awful and she was glad of it.

At camp it was different. At camp she stripped everything off the cot and made it up so tight and smooth that the counselor could bounce a quarter on it. At camp...

Nickie's eyes filled with tears. Slowly the tears overflowed and ran down her cheeks. She knelt on the bed and put her elbows on the window sill. She looked out the open window into the backyard through the branches of the sour cherry tree.

She could see Roger's horrible old car, with no top and no doors and no hood over the naked engine.

Ugh! People used to get along just fine without cars. Without cars, there would still be horses. Not just at riding stables and summer camps but everywhere, for everyone. Horses to ride, horses to pull carriages and wagons and fire engines.

Next door, at Mrs. Walton's house, the back screen door banged and a little boy, about five years old, came out.

"Corky!" Someone was calling from inside the house.

The boy looked back over his shoulder, then went straight to the trash can by the corner of the house.

"Corky!" the voice called again.

"I'm coming, I'm coming," said Corky, as he lifted the lid off the trash can and stuck one arm in — clear up to his shoulder.

"Corky!"

"All right, all right," said Corky in a calm voice, as he pulled a crooked wire coat hanger out of the trash can. Then he pulled out a coffee can, a length of string, a broken teacup, and a small empty medicine bottle. He carried them back into the house.

Nickie watched to see what would happen next. The screen door slammed again. This time a girl, about Nickie's age, came out of the house.

I can see her and she can't see me, thought Nickie. That's good. I don't have to go down if I don't want to. Nobody can make me.

The girl was wearing a T-shirt, blue jeans, and faded red sneakers. One side of her straight light hair was already braided. She was braiding the other side. Her tanned fingers flew in and out, down the whole length of the braid. She slipped a rubber band off one wrist, twisted it around the end of the braid, and tossed the braid over her shoulder.

Then she shoved her hands in her pockets and began to whistle. She whistled very well — much better than Nickie could whistle.

Nickie decided to go down after all.

Halfway down the back stairs, she stopped. She could hear her mother in the kitchen. She would be sure to say, "Now run right over and make friends with Mrs. Walton's granddaughter." She might even want to lead Nickie over by the hand!

Nickie tiptoed back up the stairs and along the hall to the front stairs. She went down quietly and out onto the wide front porch — the new front porch that had cost twice as much as a whole summer at camp. Roger had just started to paint the railings.

Nickie drifted silently around the house to the back, not looking at the yard next door. She bent to walk under the apple tree, and pulled off one of the lopsided green apples and bit into it. Ugh!

She tossed it over her shoulder and turned to see where it landed. It landed right at the feet of the girl with the pale-colored pigtails.

Looking down at her from above, Nickie had decided that the girl had blue eyes and light eyebrows — but she didn't. She had very black eyebrows and gray eyes. And she was just a little taller than Nickie.

"Hi," said Nickie.

"Hi," said the girl. "Are those apples any good?"

"No, they're awful."

"Are you Nickie?" asked the girl. "Because if you are, my grandmother says you came to my party when I was three. Isn't that funny?"

"I don't remember it," said Nickie, "but my brother does. What's your name?"

"Abigail, but they call me Gail. I'm named for my grandmother. But her friends call her Abby."

"I'm named for a grandmother too," Nickie said. "Annick. It's sort of a funny name, but my grandmother was named for *her* grandmother and she came from Holland. Say, why don't you come on over?"

If Wishes Were Horses

Gail jumped over the hedge. "Am I ever glad you're right next door — and home too!" she exclaimed. "You know how it is in the summer. Everybody's away some place."

"I'd be away too," said Nickie, "if it wasn't for termites."

"Termites?" Gail looked at her doubtfully. "Is that some kind of joke?"

"It's no joke. I was supposed to go away to camp today, but last month my father noticed that the front steps were sort of sagging. It turned out that the underneath of the porch was just loaded with termites. And some old beams under the house too. The termites had been chewing away under there for years. It's an old house, you know, and wooden.

"We had to have the old porch ripped off and a new one built and some new beams under the living room too. Boy, was it ever expensive! My father couldn't afford to have painters come then, so my brother's doing the painting. But at the rate he's going he won't live long enough to finish."

"You were pretty lucky that your father noticed the steps," Gail said.

"Lucky! I wish people would stop telling me I'm lucky! It was the *un*luckiest thing that ever happened to me because now my parents can't afford to send me to camp. If my father hadn't noticed the steps when he did — I mean, if he hadn't noticed them until six weeks later — why, I'd have been at camp by the time they found out about the termites.... See?"

Gail nodded a little uncertainly.

"Oh, well. Come and meet my brother."

By now, Roger had a little more paint on the porch railings, and a little paint on himself.

"How do you do?" said Gail, when Nickie introduced them.

"Hi," said Roger, with an amiable wave of his paintbrush. "Oops!" The waved brush sent a half circle of paint splatters across the new board floor. "Oh, well, I have to paint that anyway. You staying long?"

"I don't know," said Gail. "My father had to come to Washington to do some work for the government. He isn't sure how long it will take, so we

came along. We're staying with my grandmother for now, but we can't stay too long on account of Corky, my little brother. My grandmother likes him and all that, and I guess he likes her — but you can tell already that he would drive her stark raving crazy if we stayed too long. My mother and father are going to look for some place to rent. Near here, if they can find it."

"What's your father doing for the government?" asked Roger.

"I'm not sure," admitted Gail. "He's a mining engineer, and it has something to do with that. That's all I know."

"Well, see you around," said Roger, with another wave of his brush. "Oops!"

"By the time you finish the railings, the floor will be painted already," observed Nickie.

"Why don't you run off and find something useful to do?" demanded Roger. "Something like picking cherries so Mother'll have to make a pie."

"Oh sure, right away," replied Nickie. "And then we can watch you eat it."

As Nickie led the way around to the backyard, Gail kept looking around at everything. "I'm trying to decide if I really remember being here before," she explained. "Sometimes I think I do, and then sometimes I think I don't. I know I don't remember that," she said, pointing to Roger's old car. "Does it run?"

"Run? Hah! Do you know that every single

piece of that thing came from a different place? Like junk heaps and old wrecked cars, and those places where it says NO DUMPING ALLOWED but people dump stuff anyway. Even if Roger could get that thing to run, he isn't old enough to get a license yet."

Gail walked to the back of the yard, past the garage and the old pear tree that never had any pears on it, clear back to the high board fence.

"What's over there?" she asked.

"Oh, that's just the back of a big old place with a big old house that nobody lives in," Nickie said casually. "The front is around on Collier Drive, blocks from here. There's a high stone wall and iron gates, and it's just bristling with NO TRESPASSING signs."

"It doesn't say NO TRESPASSING here. Why don't we shin over the fence and have a look around?" Gail said eagerly, as she put both hands on top of the fence and scrabbled around for a toehold.

"There's nothing in there," insisted Nickie, pulling her back, "except poison ivy and lots of blackberries with millions and jillions of prickles. Besides, the old man who owns it is really fierce. You never know when he's going to show up, and once he caught some boys trespassing... were they ever in trouble! Say, you know what?"

"What?" asked Gail.

"That wasn't such a bad idea of Roger's — about the cherries. If we pick enough, Mother'll make two pies. Maybe three. Come on, let's get something to put them in."

Nickie ran into the kitchen, with Gail at her heels. "Mother! *Mo-ther*! Oh, there you are. Mother, if Gail and I pick gallons of cherries, will you make a pie for lunch? Maybe even before lunch? I'm starved."

"That's because —" Mrs. Baxter stopped. Nickie knew she was going to say "because you didn't eat any breakfast." But she didn't. Instead she said, "Nickie, that's a fine idea about the cherries. And, you know, I've been thinking over what Daddy said at breakfast — that you might have a kitten or a puppy. I think a kitten would be best, because of the summer rules about keeping dogs tied up. How would you like to drive over to the animal shelter this afternoon? You could pick out a kitten for your very own."

Nickie had never really thought about having a kitten before. She looked at Gail.

"I wish I could pick out a kitten for my very own," Gail said. "But we're only visiting — and we've got enough on our hands with Corky."

"Can Gail come?" asked Nickie.

"If it's all right with her mother. Here, take these little pans to pick into, and you can empty them into this big one."

Up in the branches of the old cherry tree, they pulled the soft warm cherries off in clusters and dropped them into the pans.

"That's my room up there," said Nickie, pointing. "You can get out that window onto one of the branches and climb down the tree. I used to do it a lot, but it takes about six times as long as walking down the stairs. . . . If you had just one wish — just one — that could come true, what would you wish for?"

Gail unhooked one of her pigtails from a reaching branch. "What would you wish for?" she asked.

"A horse," breathed Nickie. "A horse of my very own. What would you wish for?"

Gail said slowly, "Maybe you'll think it's silly. But if I had one wish, just one, I'd wish for curly hair."

Nickie nearly fell out of the tree with surprise. Was Gail going to turn out to be one of those dopey girls who spends all her time looking in mirrors and doing her hair different ways and snitching lipstick? She didn't seem like that kind of girl.

"What good is curly hair?" asked Nickie.

"Oh, you can say that. Sure. You've *got* curly hair. You can keep it short so it doesn't get in your eyes when you go swimming. I bet you just pull a comb through it once, and you're through for the day. Look at mine. Just look at it. I had it short once and it was terrible. Just strings, flopping.

Now it's long and it takes forever to brush it and comb it and braid it. Besides, I get tired listening to people talk about it. 'What a shame,' they say, 'her mother has such lovely hair. Wouldn't you just know it would be the little boy that would get the curls?' Ugh!"

Nickie ran her hand thoughtfully over her own short curls. Gail made sense, in a way.

"Maybe you're right," she admitted. "Just the same, I absolutely cannot imagine wasting my wish on something like curly hair when I could have a horse for it instead!"

To Give Away

The pies — three of them, deep and wide and simply loaded with red cherries — didn't get into the oven until nearly lunchtime. Then Gail's mother called her to come home for lunch.

After lunch, Roger burned his mouth sampling one of the pies. "Wow! Nothing is as hot as the inside of a cherry pie unless it's the inside of a boiled onion!"

"Get away from those pies!" scolded his mother. "If you cut them hot, they tear all to pieces and it makes me mad. I didn't crimp that fancy crust to have you scramble it up like shredded wheat. Go paint the porch until the pies cool. Nickie, run and get Gail. We'll drive over to the animal shelter and have cherry pie when we get back."

But when Nickie knocked on Mrs. Walton's

back door, Gail reported sadly that she couldn't come. "Mother and Dad found this ad in the paper and they've gone to look at a house. I have to keep an eye on Corky. You ought to see what he dragged into the kitchen this morning while Grandmother was busy upstairs!"

"Bring him along," invited Nickie. "If your mother won't mind."

"Oh, *my* mother won't mind," said Gail. "And sometimes he's a perfect angel, especially with strangers."

Nickie and Gail sat in the front seat of the car with Mrs. Baxter, and Corky sat silently in the back. He had Gail's silvery-gold hair, except that *his* was curly, and he had the same surprising black eyebrows and gray eyes.

The animal shelter was only about a mile out in the country. The suburbs were closing in on it, though. In what used to be cow pastures, there were rows and rows of flat-topped houses all just exactly alike.

"I'm glad we live in an old house, with an attic and a basement and a pointed roof," observed Nickie. "Even if the old porch did get eaten up."

"I like your house," said Gail. "I hope we find one just like it to rent. And close too."

The animal shelter was a long low building, with fenced-in runs for dogs beside it. As Mrs. Baxter parked the car, every single dog came bounding and barking up to the fences. The cats and kittens were inside, in small wire cages.

"A kitten for the little girl?" repeated the woman in the office. "Yes, indeed, we have some lovely kittens. Many of them are not strays at all, especially this time of year."

"Why this time of year?" asked Nickie.

"People go away for their vacations," answered the woman in a tired voice. "They drop their pets off here, expecting us to find good homes for them."

"What happens if you don't find good homes for them?" asked Nickie, and then she was sorry she had asked. She already knew the answer.

"It's worse than the old man in *Millions of Cats*!" groaned Gail, as they wandered back and forth in front of the cages. "Every single kitten is the prettiest."

"And I ought to know," chanted Corky, "because I've seen hundreds of cats, thousands of cats, millions and billions and trillions of cats!"

The woman in charge looked at Corky over her glasses. "Young man," she remarked, "you and I have a good deal in common."

At last Nickie decided. "Oh, this is the one, I just know it. Look at his face, like a striped pansy! He's a darling."

She squeezed her fingers in through the wire, and the kitten bunted his hard little head up against them, purring so wildly that he shook all over. He was a warm pinkish-tan, with dark tortoise-shell markings. When he rolled over on his back, his fat little stomach turned out to be a paler shade of tan, covered with blurry speckles like a baby robin's.

"This is the one," said Nickie firmly. "I absolutely am not going to even glance at another kitten!"

The woman lifted the kitten out of the cage and carried him, still purring, into the office.

"Where's Corky?" asked Gail suddenly. "Yikes! I better find him."

She dashed back into the room with the cat cages. No Corky. Nickie left her mother signing the adoption papers, and ran outside with Gail.

Corky was not sitting in the car. Nickie and Gail ran around the building, each in a different direction. They met in the back. No Corky.

Behind the building, some distance away, stood a couple of sheds and a parked truck with a wire-mesh gate across the back. Beyond, a hillside of scattered trees and bushes came down nearly to the sheds.

Nickie ran to the sheds. Gail ran over to the truck.

"Here he is!" shouted Gail. "Corcoran Walton, you come out of that truck, right this very minute!"

"I can't," replied Corky in a satisfied voice. "I'm locked in."

"Oh, for Pete's sake!" Gail shook the gate. "I don't think it's locked at all. It's only stuck. I'll get you out of there. *Nickie*!"

Nickie didn't hear. She was standing outside one of the sheds, a sort of three-sided lean-to, looking in. She was looking at a horse, a dusty, dark-colored horse that was tied to the doorpost. The horse's head hung down; he whisked at the flies with a quick swish of his tail and heaved a long, noisy sigh.

An elderly man with a kind, serious face came around the shed with a bucket of water, which he set down in front of the horse.

"Oh, please," gasped Nickie, nearly choking on the words. "Does this horse belong to anybody, or is he to give away like the dogs and cats?"

"Oh, please!" cried Gail, dashing up, out of breath. Can you come and help me? My little brother is stuck in your truck."

The man slowly straightened up, his face crinkling into a smile. "One at a time," he begged. "One at a time. This old horse, now. He's just a poor old stray, wandered off from wherever he rightfully belongs. Might be his folks just turned him loose to get lost. Some folks are just as mean as that. Now, miss, let's see to this little boy. It does beat all what a little boy can think up to do, don't it? But don't you worry, he can't harm that old truck."

"I wouldn't be too sure," said Gail ominously, as

they went off together toward the truck.

Nickie reached out and stroked the horse's nose as he lifted it, dripping, from the water bucket. She stepped into the shed and ran her hand along his side. She could feel every one of his big ribs. He shifted his weight on his feet and put his head down. He looked as if he had been standing for a long, long time.

"You don't belong to anybody," whispered Nickie fiercely. "You could belong to me."

But it wouldn't do any good to ask. She had asked it so often already: "Even if you can't afford to buy me a horse, what if I could get one free? What if I won one in a contest, then would you let me keep it?"

She knew all the answers: "Do you know that in this town a homeowner must have two acres of land to keep a horse? Do you have any idea what it costs to board a horse at a riding stable? Do you have any idea how much work there is to taking care of a horse? Now, for the last time, Nickie, the answer is no, and we don't want to hear another word about it."

All right, then. They wouldn't hear another word about it. Nickie looked toward the truck. Gail and the old man were having trouble opening the gate.

With quick, shaking fingers, Nickie untied the knot around the doorpost. With the rope over her shoulder, she took a couple of steps. The horse

obediently took a couple of steps behind her. He would lead like a lamb. Quickly she retied the rope.

"Not now," Nickie whispered to the horse. "Not yet."

She ran her hand down his nose, around his muzzle. The horse, like the kitten, leaned his head against her stroking hands. She was talking softly to him all the time.

"Take a good look at me. Listen to my voice. You'll know me again, won't you?"

She turned away from the shed just as Corky jumped down from the truck, and her mother came out of the building carrying the kitten.

A Secret Place

The cherry pies were just right for eating — not too hot and not too cooled off. Roger had already eaten half of one. Mrs. Baxter, Nickie, Gail, and Corky sat around the kitchen table and ate the other half. Then they ate half of another pie.

Corky wiped his mouth on the back of his wrist and said thoughtfully, "There's a whole pie and a half left over. What do you do at your house with leftover pies?"

"*Corky*!" exclaimed Gail. "He isn't old enough to have any manners yet," she apologized to Mrs. Baxter.

"I have too got manners!" cried Corky indignantly. He pushed his chair back and walked over to the back door. "Thank you for the pie," he said politely. "I liked it a lot. I like it better with vanilla ice cream," he added, marching out and letting the screen door slam.

Gail ran after him, but she was back in a few minutes. "Mother's home. The house was no good, only two bedrooms. Imagine if I had to share a room with Corky!"

"He seems a cheerful little fellow," said Mrs. Baxter.

"Oh, he's cheerful enough," said Gail. "It's not that. It's that he takes everything apart. Doorknobs, egg beaters, water faucets, roller skates, radios — everything. He doesn't break them, you understand. He's very careful about that. My father says that if there was just one screw holding the universe together, Corky would find it and unscrew it and — bingo!"

Mrs. Baxter got a faraway look in her eyes. "Your father should have known Roger when he was five years old," she murmured.

Nickie and Gail washed the dishes and then took the kitten outdoors. Nickie led the way to a grassy place behind the garage, a very private place that nobody could see unless they looked around the corner of the garage.

She sat down on the grass and the kitten started kneading fiercely at her lap.

"Oh, let me hold him a minute," begged Gail.

"Here. Take him. Listen, Gail, you don't like horses very much, do you?"

"What a peculiar thing to say!" exclaimed Gail.

"Why would anybody *not* like horses?"

"Then, you do like them?"

"Sure, I like them. I love to ride."

"I just wanted to make sure. Listen. Did you notice that horse at the animal shelter?"

"Well, not very carefully. I was worried about Corky. That horse looked pretty old and broken down, though, didn't he?"

"He did not! Maybe he wasn't exactly young, but somebody's been starving that horse! You ought to feel his ribs. But he's not a bit mean or bad-tempered. He's just as gentle and friendly — and he liked me. Gail, you know what happens to animals at that place if nobody claims them or offers them a home? You do know, don't you?"

"Yes," said Gail uncomfortably. "They — they put them out of their misery. It sounds terrible, I know. But really, Nickie, it's better than letting them starve to death, or get sick and die."

"That's what people think. But do they care what the animals think? That horse wouldn't have any misery to be put out of if somebody took half-way decent care of him. And they're not going to keep him around the animal shelter for long — you can tell that. They don't have any place for horses. That old shed is where they keep the truck; there were big grease spots on the floor."

"But, golly, Nickie, there isn't anything you can do about it," protested Gail. "The best thing is just not to think about it."

"I will think about it!" flared Nickie. "And I'll do something about it too! I'm going to take that horse away from there before it's too late. Tonight, in the middle of the night."

"*Nickie*!" exclaimed Gail in horror. "That would be stealing."

"You just tell me who I'd be stealing from," Nickie demanded. "Who? Tell me that. Whoever owned him doesn't want him or they'd have phoned the animal shelter by now. The animal shelter doesn't want him. You know what they're going to do with him. Well, all right, *I* want him!"

Gail stared at her. Nickie's face was pale under her tan. "Jeepers," whispered Gail. "I really believe you mean it. But will your folks let you keep a horse?"

Nickie frowned. "Wait here a minute," she said, and picked up the kitten and took him back to the house.

When she returned, she said to Gail in a low voice, "I'm going to show you something. I'd have shown you before but it's a secret, and it's not just my secret. There are four of us, and we're not supposed to tell anybody unless we all four say so. But the other three are away, so I'm going to break the rules. Only you must promise on your honor never, never to tell anybody else."

"All right," said Gail breathlessly.

"Then say, 'I promise on my honor,' " insisted Nickie.

"I promise on my honor," repeated Gail.

"Then follow me, and be as quiet as you can."

Nickie strolled over to the back fence. The garage was between her and the back windows of her own house. The thick upshooting branches of the old pear tree blocked any view from Gail's grandmother's house.

Nickie squatted down and picked up a short strong stick that was lying in the grass at the bottom of the fence. "We keep this here," she whispered. "Nobody thinks anything about it."

With the stick, she pried up one of the wide upright fence boards. When the board lifted clear of the ground, Nickie put her hand under it and pushed upward. The board slid up, leaving an oblong opening at the bottom of the fence.

"Quick, wiggle through," she whispered. "Then hold it for me. Watch out for the poison ivy."

Gail crawled through, then held the heavy board while Nickie squeezed through. When she let it go, it dropped into place with a soft thud. Nobody on the other side could tell that there was a way here to get through the fence.

Gail, on her hands and knees, was pinned against the fence by whippy green vines and dry weeds. They were so thick above her head that she couldn't stand up.

"We used to go over the fence," Nickie whispered. "But they can see you on the top, and jumping down was making a big bare place on this side. Stay down, we still have to crawl. I'll go first."

Nickie parted a thick curtain of Virginia creeper and crawled beneath it. Gail followed, keeping her eyes on the soles of Nickie's sneakers. It was a regular tunnel. Stems and branches and leaves made a green wall all around her, but hardly any of them reached out and grabbed at her as she crawled along. The ground under her hands and knees was worn smooth and bare.

After perhaps thirty or forty feet, Nickie stood up. Gail stood up. A narrow twisting path opened up ahead through young trees and saplings, all overgrown and bound together with honeysuckle and Virginia creeper.

"We can walk the rest of the way," said Nickie softly, "but don't talk out loud. Yet."

On silent sneakers they followed the path. It sloped upward, but not steeply. After a while, big trees appeared and the underbrush thinned out in their dense shade.

Nickie stepped around the base of a huge spreading oak, picking her way over the mossy roots that twisted out in every direction. Gail followed, and they stepped out into checkered sunlight.

"Well, here we are," said Nickie in her normal voice. "What do you think of it?"

Gail stared. The big oak spread out and out until its farthest branches reached down and touched the shingled roof of an old building. It was two buildings really — joined in an L-shape — a stable and a carriage house. Along one side of the L stretched six empty stalls with a tack room behind them. Along the other side, the old carriage house stood high and wide and square. Once you could have driven two carriages abreast through the open doorway. Above the carriage house was the hayloft, where an old block and tackle still dangled from the big window. Beyond the buildings stood a second giant oak.

"Well," repeated Nickie. "What do you think of it?"

"It's wonderful," whispered Gail. "It's beautiful. It's hard to believe."

"You can talk out loud now," Nickie said. "Nobody can hear us here. Nobody can even get here except me and Mollie and Joan and Debby. And now you."

"But this is a stable," said Gail. "I thought you said it was an old house."

"The house is up there, farther on. We don't go there. Sometimes people come there, but they don't come here. They can't."

"How do you mean, they can't? There must have been a drive once. Nobody would have stables they couldn't get to."

"Oh sure, there used to be a drive. You can still

see the gravel under the weeds, but we fixed it so nobody would want to get through."

"How?" asked Gail. But Nickie ignored the question.

"Look," she said, "let's not stand around out here. Come on in and see how we fixed up the inside."

Two Will Go

Nickie led the way through the empty carriage house to a ladder at the back, and then up through a square hole in the ceiling to the hayloft.

High over their heads the roof beams curved to a point, like the ceiling of a church. The air was still, and smelled faintly of long-gone hay and warm wooden boards. Near the big hayloft window at the back, there were some faded cushions to sit on and stacks of comic books and a bookcase made from an old orange crate. Gail read some of the titles in the bookcase: *Heads Up, Heels Down; The Secret Garden; National Velvet; The Complete Horseman's Encyclopedia.*

Everything was so exactly right that Gail could not think of anything to say about it. Finally she just said, "Neat."

"Yes, isn't it?" Nickie agreed proudly. "You should have seen it before we fixed it up though. Here, have a seat."

They sat down on the cushions.

"Why don't people come here? You didn't tell me," Gail reminded her.

"Oh, that. It's because of the poison ivy. There wasn't a bit on the place when we first started coming here years ago — well, three years anyway — so we transplanted some. Put on gloves, long sleeves, long pants, high socks — the works. We dug up basketfuls and planted it where it would show the most. We planted some down by our fence too, where we came in. Roger gets poison ivy like crazy. It's all spread beautifully too."

Gail gave a long admiring whistle. "Jeepers. Didn't any of you catch it?"

"I hardly get poison ivy, even if I touch it, and neither does Joan. But Mollie and Deb did. Wow! Their mothers couldn't imagine how they caught it. Now, look, I want to ask you something." Nickie hugged her knees, frowning. "Now that you've seen our secret place, don't you think I could keep a horse here? I could, couldn't I? Well, couldn't I?"

Gail thought about it seriously.

"You'd have to figure on so many things," she said at last. "Is there any place to get water? I mean, nearer than your house. Water's terribly heavy to carry. Then there's feed. And exercise. And you'd be surprised how often horses get sick, or hurt themselves. There'd be vet's bills and of course you'd have to get the horse here in the first place."

"I'll get him here, don't you worry," said Nickie grimly. "I'll worry about the other things later. I'll have to bring him in the front way and I don't like to do that because someone might see us and start asking questions. But in the middle of the night, the very darkest middle of the night...once I'm through the gates, the rest will be easy."

She jumped up and headed for the ladder. "I'd better check the way down from the house to the stables while it's light. Come on."

Nickie skirted the stables and started up the slope behind them. Beyond the shade of the big oaks, the jungle of vines and saplings sprang up again. As Nickie pushed and shoved her way through, she trampled down a path.

"I hate to do this, but it'll grow together again. Oops! Poison ivy. Watch it."

The underbrush thinned out and suddenly the house, surrounded by crooked evergreens and straggly rhododendrons, loomed up ahead of them.

Gail ran across the creaking side porch and peered in at a narrow window. "Why, it looks all right inside," she said in a disappointed voice. "Furniture and everything. I thought it would be all cobwebby and — and *haunted.*"

"I told you the owner comes here sometimes. Mr. Olds, that's his name. Then there's another man, a sort of caretaker. He comes quite often, opens the windows, takes a look around, and all that. We've watched him, but he's never seen us. He has somebody mow the lawn about once a year too. Not with lawnmowers — with those big machines they use to cut hay. They even had the house painted a couple of years ago. We hid all our stuff and kept away until the painters were through."

"It's a funny-looking house, but I sort of like it," said Gail. "All those different-shaped windows and porches, and lightning rods all over the roof. I never saw anything like this in Colorado. You'd think the owner would be glad to live in it."

"Oh, he has stacks of houses, I guess. He's not only old and mean, he's rich too. I mean really rich. This used to be his country place, way out beyond all the other houses, when it was built. Now look, you can see the front gates from here."

The drive, after circling the house, stretched away downhill through acres of tall, wild-looking grass to the big iron gates. On either side of the gates there was a high stone wall enclosing the property.

"Are the gates locked?" asked Gail.

"Yes. Padlock as big as your head. The caretaker uses a key, but that's a laugh. On one side the hinges are rusted right through. I can drag it open enough to slide through. I did it once."

"And slide a horse through too?" asked Gail.

"I can if I have to. And I'll have to, that's all. Let's go back. It's almost suppertime and I've got a lot of things to think about."

They went back around the house and down the freshly trampled path to the stables.

"Do you suppose there's somebody at the animal shelter all night?" asked Gail.

"I don't know. Maybe that man who helped you get Corky out of the truck. But he wouldn't stay awake all night, would he? He'd have to get some sleep."

They kept going, past the stables.

"What if the dogs bark?" asked Gail suddenly.

"That's one of the things I'm thinking about," replied Nickie soberly.

They reached the tunnel in the underbrush and crawled through. Nickie pried up the board in the fence and peered under.

"Okay," she whispered.

She squeezed through and Gail followed.

Nickie lay flat on her back on the grass behind the garage and closed her eyes. "I'm trying to think of everything ahead of time," she explained.

Gail lay down beside her.

"How are you going to wake up?" she asked.

"Alarm clock under my pillow."

"And climb down the cherry tree?"

"No. Walk out the front door. Quietly."

"If it was me, I'd climb down the tree," said Gail.

"This isn't a game of cops and robbers I'm playing," said Nickie scornfully. "It's slow and scratchy in that tree, and I've never done it in the dark. Besides, some of the branches reach across Roger's window and they might scrape on the screen and wake him up."

"I see. I guess I wasn't thinking."

"Well, I'm thinking. This is for real."

After a while, Gail said slowly, "If this is for real, and not just something to do for kicks, why go to all the bother of stealing a horse? Why not just ask for the horse? Wouldn't that make more sense?"

"You don't understand," said Nickie patiently. "I'm not just stirring up trouble for myself. You can't just say, 'Give me a horse,' and walk away with it. There are rules. Some grown-up has to sign papers, promising to take care of the animal you pick out, and my father and mother would never, never sign a paper for me to have a horse."

"How do you know?" persisted Gail. "Did you ever ask them for a horse?"

"Only about a hundred thousand million times, and they have exactly a hundred thousand million reasons why not. Good reasons too," added Nickie, making a face.

"But there never was a horse that you could adopt before," Gail pointed out. "Now there is. So why not ask them again? They might say yes. And if they said no, what could you lose?"

"What could I lose? Only the horse, that's all. If I ask them, they'll know that there is a horse at the shelter and that I want it. Then, say that horse turns up missing. Suppose they happen to find out about it. Who's the first person they're going to ask about that horse? Me, that's who. And another thing: Where's the first place they'd think of looking for that horse? You know where."

"But the stables are a secret, aren't they?" asked Gail.

"Well, yes. But lots of people know that there used to be stables at the Olds' place. And my mother knows that we used to go over the fence and play around in there, but she never really gives it a thought. So what happens to the secret if hordes of people start tramping around in there looking for a lost horse? And what would Mollie and Joan and Deb say when they came back and found everything all spoiled? Now do you see?"

"Yes, I see. I guess you have figured it all out," said Gail.

"Yes, I have," replied Nickie.

"Well, then, I'll come with you."

Nickie rolled over on her stomach and stared at Gail. "What?"

"I said, I'll come with you. Tonight. Two people will make it more sure. You never know with a horse, and that's a heavy gate to open. What do you think will be the best time to start?"

"Really, Gail? Really, you'll come with me? Oh,

am I glad! It will be awfully dark. I wasn't scared about coming back, because then there would be two of us — me and the horse. But going all alone, all by myself!"

"Now there will be two of us going," said Gail, "And three coming back."

"But are you perfectly sure? What if you get caught?"

"Well, what if *you* get caught?" replied Gail. "Besides, what could they do to us, really?"

"Take the horse away," muttered Nickie. "But we won't get caught. I won't let us get caught. We'll start about one. It gets light early in June, and we've got plenty to do before then. But we mustn't start until everybody's sound asleep."

"How will I wake up?" asked Gail suddenly. "I don't have an alarm clock."

"I'll lend you Roger's. He'll never miss it, with no school. Besides, he sleeps like a log until somebody comes and throws him out of bed."

Then the back door slammed, and they heard Roger shouting, "*Nickie! Supper!*"

"Call again," they heard Mrs. Baxter say. "She's off somewhere with the little girl from next door."

"NICKIE!" Roger bellowed.

"Got to go now," whispered Nickie. "See you later. I'll bring you the clock after supper, and we'll decide about where to meet. *Coming!*" she shouted, and ran around the garage to the house.

The Middle of the Night

The bedroom door opened a crack and the light from the hall sliced across Nickie's bed. She lay on her side, her dark lashes quiet on her cheeks, one ear buried in the pillow and one arm curled around the sleeping kitten.

"They always look like angels when they're asleep," murmured her mother. "I wonder — do you think that kitten should go down to the basement? What about fleas?"

"Oh, let it stay," said her father. "If that kitten can take her mind off horses, let it sleep where it likes — fleas and all."

The door closed quietly. Nickie kept her eyes shut until she heard her parents' door click shut down the hall. Then her eyes flew open in the dark.

Inside her head she went over the plan again,

step by step and block by block. The first three blocks would be the most ticklish; they were long blocks, solidly built up with houses. The houses were old, with old trees whose arching branches almost blotted out the streetlights, and this made the sidewalk a dark and scary place at night.

After three blocks the houses thinned out and the sidewalks ended. There would be vacant lots to cut through from street to street. One of these streets came to a dead end at the top of the slope behind the animal shelter. At the bottom of that slope was the shed. The horse was in the shed, and his rope halter was fastened with a knot that Nickie herself had tied.

Coming back, they would have to make a wide circle to avoid the houses. It would be much longer, but safer with the horse. The roundabout way would take them nearly to the edges of Rock Creek Park. They would have one little stretch of sidewalks and houses and then — the stone wall and the iron gate of the Olds' place.

Nickie let out a sigh and tightened her arm around the kitten, who began to purr gustily. He made more noise than the little clock ticking away under her pillow.

She pulled the clock out and looked at its glowing hands. A few minutes after eleven. Nearly two more hours to wait.

What a long, strange, crowded day it had been. A new friend. A new kitten.

What a long, strange, busy night it was going to be. A new horse . . .

Rrrrrrrrrrrr . . .

Nickie reached under her pillow and choked off the alarm almost before she was awake.

She lay still, listening.

Not a sound. Nobody had heard.

A muscle at a time, she slid out of bed and moved with outstretched hands to the closet door. Inside, on the floor, lay her flashlight, blue sneakers, navy blue pullover with long sleeves, and her darkest blue jeans. One pocket of the jeans was bulgy with lump sugar.

Silently she shed her pajamas and dressed by touch. Then she picked up the flashlight and moved along the wall to the hall door. She slid her fingers around the doorknob and began to turn it.

Something bumped against her ankle, and she nearly shouted with surprise and fright.

"Mrrrrrow!"

The kitten. She had forgotten the kitten.

"Meeow!"

"Ssh," she breathed soundlessly, picking him up. He would have to go down in the basement after all.

She eased the door open and closed it again gently. With the kitten cuddled under her chin, she tiptoed down the back stairs to the kitchen, where the tiny pilot lights on the stove made a faint blue glow on the walls and ceiling.

She opened the door to the basement. It squeaked. She put the kitten on the top step and closed the door. It squeaked again.

She stood still, listening.

There was nothing to hear except the *thup, thup, thup* of the kitten's feet as he ventured down the basement steps.

Nickie thought about the back door, so close she could almost touch it. But she would have to step off the back porch onto the crunchy gravel of the driveway. She moved instead through the dining room and front hall to the front door. It was a good door, heavy and silent.

She pushed the button that released the lock and closed the door after her.

It was a lucky thing Roger was so slow with his painting. Only part of the railing and two pillars had wet paint on them. The new porch floor was solid and quiet. The new steps were solid and quiet.

Nickie drifted like a shadow across the front lawn to the black bulk of the big forsythia bush in the corner.

Gail was already there. She too was wearing dark clothes. Her face and hair were a pale blur in the darkness.

They touched hands without a word, and Nickie quickly led the way along the sidewalk. Gail followed so silently that several times Nickie looked back to make sure she was really there.

Here and there an upstairs window glowed faintly — perhaps a night light in some child's room. They came to the end of the first block and crossed the street.

In the middle of the second block a dog barked. Nickie's heart missed a beat, but the dog did not come rushing and jumping at them. Perhaps he was tied in the backyard or closed in the garage. They kept on going, and the barking died away behind them and finally stopped. They slipped across the next street and started down the third block.

Up ahead, a porch light suddenly came on. Voices called out. Somebody laughed, loud in the sleeping night. A car door slammed. It was a late dinner party breaking up.

Another car door slammed and headlights streamed down the street. A car engine started.

Nickie grabbed Gail's arm and together they moved back from the sidewalk, back across somebody's front lawn, back into the prickly evergreens by somebody's front door. A car backed and turned, the headlights raking in a wide circle across the house fronts. Nickie and Gail froze, as still as still, among the scratchy branches.

One car drove past, then another. A last car started up and drove the other way, its red tail-lights dwindling down the street. At the house the front door banged shut and the porch light went off.

They waited for one long minute, and then went on. At the end of the block a cat crossed the street in front of them, a dark moving blur with two gleaming eyes.

Now the houses were fewer and farther apart. The streetlights were farther apart too, and dimmer. Nickie cut through the vacant lots until they came to the dead-end street they wanted. They followed it past the last house, past the last streetlight.

Now there was uneven ground under their feet, and grass and weeds. They were at the top of the hill that led down to the animal shelter.

Suddenly Nickie's knees let go and she sat down on the ground. Gail sat down too. They had come all this way without saying one single word to each other.

"Well, we made it this far," whispered Nickie.

Away from the streetlights, their eyes slowly got used to the darkness. They could see the black shape of every tree and bush on the hillside below. They could see the dark outline of the animal shelter and the sheds behind it. Away to the south the pinkish glow of the city lit up the edge of the sky.

Finally Gail whispered, "We can't sit here all night."

"I know. Perhaps I'd better go up to the horse by myself. He knows me, a little. You wait back a ways."

"All right. Don't move suddenly and startle him. He might neigh, or kick out and make a racket."

"I know. I won't. Here, take the flashlight. I'll need both hands."

Slowly, carefully, quietly, they picked their way down the slope. Nickie's heart was beating so hard she could feel it in the top of her head. Almost before she was ready to be there, she was standing on the level ground behind the shed.

Through the Gate

Inside the shed the horse stamped one foot lightly and made a loud breathing noise, a sort of whiffle.

Suddenly Nickie felt all right — perfectly calm and ordinary. She walked steadily and silently around the shed, reaching in her pocket for a handful of sugar.

She stepped into the darkness of the shed, moving one hand up the rope that held the horse and holding the other hand out, palm full of sugar lumps.

The horse stirred, shifted his feet. She felt a gust of warm breath on her wrist and palm as the sugar was lipped off. Nickie untied the horse, shortened her grip on the rope, and walked slowly out of the shed. The horse followed obediently. There was a soft clop, clop of hoofs on packed earth, until they reached the silent grass. Nickie started up the slope at a slant, bent forward, with the rope over her shoulder.

Gail, walking to one side, tripped over a root and made a little startled noise as she fell. Behind them, a dog yapped sharply. Then a hound bayed. Then the whole chorus broke loose.

Nickie called, "You all right?"

"Yes. *Hurry*!"

Nickie hurried, walking as fast as she could uphill. The horse came along willingly enough. Almost too willingly; his head was crowding her shoulder. She spoke to him quietly, and he seemed to hear in spite of the racket. "Steady, boy. Take it easy, fellow. Easy does it."

As one dog after another gave up, the chorus slacked off and became a scattering of yaps and barks and howls. One last dog barked steadily for another long minute, then he too quit.

At the top of the hill, Nickie stopped to catch her breath. She fed the horse the rest of the sugar and let him reach down and grab a few mouthfuls of grass.

"I didn't see any watchman down there," whispered Gail. "Did you?"

"No, but he probably wouldn't come out unless the dogs barked."

"I bet the dogs bark all the time at nothing and he's used to it," Gail said confidently.

"Just the same, we better not hang around here."

They went the long way around, keeping clear of houses and streetlights as much as possible. They stumbled along over ruts they couldn't see. Where the surface was sandy, they sank in over their sneaker tops; in places they slogged through sticky, heavy clay.

Several times Gail took the rope as Nickie scouted ahead to check the route. Once she thought she was completely lost, but the glow in the sky told her which direction was south, and she soon came to a familiar corner.

"We used to bike through here in the spring," she said to Gail. "But it was daytime then."

"We're wasting a perfectly good horse," grumbled Gail. "We ought to both ride. There's stones and dirt and I don't know what all in my sneakers."

"Mine too," said Nickie. "But we're getting close. This road ought to run into Collier Drive about a block from the Olds' place. I hope."

It did. They were soon on the paved Drive, back with sidewalks and houses. Nickie slowed down until she was barely moving and led the horse along the grass strip between the sidewalk and the street. They had to weave in and out between the trees. The horse put his feet down slowly and deliberately, almost as though he knew he mustn't let his hooves ring out on the cement.

Now the last corner. The high stone wall loomed ahead. Nickie pulled the horse across the last street, around the corner onto the grass, and backed him up against the dark bulk of the wall.

"Collier is a through street," she whispered. "Trucks use it a lot and we'd show up like crazy in their headlights. You hold him and I'll go and get the gate open."

She hurried back to the corner and followed the wall down to the gate. She had barely reached it when she saw headlights coming down Collier Drive. She flattened herself against the gatepost as a car shot by with a whine and a snarl.

When the taillights of the car had disappeared, Nickie started to work on the gate. She pulled on the hinged side of the rusted gate, but it only scraped back and forth on the stone gatepost; the bottom would not move. She would have to lift and pull at the same time. She reached down for a better grip on the rusted bar, and lifted and pulled with all her might.

The heavy gate scraped back two inches, three inches, and stuck. Lift as she might, pull as she might, the gate refused to budge another inch. It was just too heavy. Or she was just too tired. Nickie gave the gate an angry kick and only hurt her toes in the canvas sneakers.

Half crying, she started back along the wall. Her throat hurt and her feet hurt and her hands hurt. And now, after all the planning and working and hoping, she couldn't get the gate open.

Another set of headlights loomed up ahead. Nickie fell flat on the grass and lay still as a trailer truck rumbled past with a roar and a whoosh. Then she picked herself up and went on around the corner to Gail and the horse.

"It's no use," she whispered hoarsely. "I can't open it far enough. Now what'll we do? *What'll we do*? There's no other way in, no other way at all that you could take a horse."

"Let me try," said Gail.

"If I couldn't, you can't. I tell you it's too heavy, and the bars are stuck at the bottom and cars keep coming by — "

"Take the rope," ordered Gail. "And the flashlight." She disappeared into the darkness.

Nickie leaned against the wall, swallowing hard to keep from crying. She ought to be thinking, planning something else, but she was too tired. The horse was cropping grass contentedly. He had followed them so trustingly, and now what would become of him? And they were so close, just the width of the wall away — just twelve inches away.

"Come on," said Gail, suddenly right beside her. Nickie jumped. "I got it open. I'll go back to the corner and watch for headlights. If there aren't any, I'll whistle."

After a minute Gail gave a low whistle, and Nickie pulled on the rope once more. The horse snatched one last mouthful of grass and followed.

Up to the corner, around the corner up to the gate. Nickie felt the width of the opening. It felt as wide as a horse.

As she started through, the horse jerked his head back sharply and stopped.

"Come on!" begged Nickie. "You can't come this far and shy at a gate. Do you *want* to be put out of your misery?"

"Here comes another car!" cried Gail. "Pull hard."

Nickie pulled with all her might while Gail gave the horse a hard slap on the rump and shouted "Hup!" He went through the gate with a rush.

Headlights flashed by on the street, throwing the barred shadow of the gate across the three of them — but they were safely inside.

Nickie was so limp with relief that she simply stood stroking the horse on the neck, and let Gail drag the heavy gate back into place.

"Gee, you sure are strong," Nickie said.

"I look skinny, but I'm tough," replied Gail. "Everybody says so. If you have an older brother, he gets the heavy chores. But if your brother is younger, you get them."

Together they led the horse up the long winding drive and around the house. Now it was safe to use a light. Nickie went ahead with the flashlight and found the trail she had trampled out. She guided Gail and the horse through it, and down to the stable yard.

Nickie threw the flashlight beam across the row of stalls, thinking about which one to use. Suddenly the horse tossed his head back, taking Gail by surprise, and jerked the rope from her hand. With a soft whinny, he walked directly into the square box stall at the end and nosed around in the empty manger.

"Well, look at that!" exclaimed Gail.

"He hasn't spent all his life in some old greasy shed," said Nickie proudly. "He knows about stables. He likes it here. That's good. Oh, I'm *so* tired. And look — it's going to be morning pretty soon."

She snapped off the flashlight. She could see Gail's face, pale and gray, by the faint light from the eastern sky.

"Gee, I hate to leave him here without anything to eat or drink," said Nickie.

"He'll be all right. He's been grabbing grass and leaves all the way here," said Gail. She tied the rope securely and gave the horse an affectionate thump on the rump. "He's no beauty, but he's sure been a gentleman tonight."

Nickie opened her mouth to say, "He is too a beauty," but a yawn came out instead.

"Let's get back before someone finds we're gone," said Gail. "Lead the way."

Single file, stumbling a little from weariness, they moved along the twisty path. Somewhere nearby a cardinal tuned up the first two notes of his song. A mockingbird chirred in answer.

Nickie and Gail crawled stiffly through the tunnel, lifted the fence board with a great effort, and tumbled through into the Baxters' backyard.

They looked at each other and grinned. Gail clasped her hands high above her head in a sign of victory.

"See you tomorrow," she whispered. "I mean, today." Then she slid through the hedge, and slipped without a sound through her grandmother's back door.

Nickie walked slowly around to the front of her house. Every minute the sky got lighter and lighter, a strange, flat, eerie light. Birds were tuning up in every tree. Soon they would all burst together into their morning chorus.

One heavy foot at a time, Nickie dragged herself up the porch steps, across the landing and through the door. She remembered to release the lock before she closed the door.

The kitten, she thought. I ought to go down in the basement and get the kitten. But she was just too tired. I'll say he bothered me in the night and I put him down there. It's the truth too.

Hand over hand on the banister rail, she pulled herself up the stairs. She opened her bedroom door and closed it silently behind her.

What was it the kids yelled when they played hide-and-seek? "Safe home!"

She was safe home.

She pulled off her clothes and fumbled her way into her pajamas, leaving the jacket unbuttoned. Mustn't leave the muddy clothes out in plain sight. She pushed them under her bed.

The light through the window was just changing from gray to pink as Nickie fell into bed. She pulled the sheet up over her face and was instantly asleep.

Highboy

When Nickie finally opened her eyes and stretched herself awake, it was nearly eleven o'clock.

It took her a minute to start remembering. It was more a feeling than a remembering, and it was a sudden all-over feeling, like falling off a dock.

She whispered it softly to herself: "I have a horse."

Oh, there was so much to do! Get up to the stables with water. Do something about feed. And find Gail. But first, the muddy clothes under the bed. She couldn't just dump them in the hamper for her mother to start asking questions about.

Mrs. Baxter was running the vacuum cleaner somewhere downstairs. Roger ought to be out painting the porch. Nickie took the clothes into the bathroom and locked the door. She rinsed them out in the bathtub, sneakers and all, and rolled them in towels to get most of the water out. Then she took a fast shower herself.

She carried the damp clothes back to her room. The sneakers could dry out under the bed, and the other things on hangers far back in the closet.

Nickie put on clean clothes and an old pair of shoes, and ran down the back stairs. Her place was still set for breakfast at the kitchen table.

She was starved, and no wonder. Hastily she shook out an enormous bowl of cereal, sliced a banana over it, and poured herself a big glass of milk.

Her mother looked into the kitchen and said, "Gail has been over looking for you. She took the kitten to play with."

"Why didn't you wake me?" asked Nickie, shoveling large spoonfuls into her mouth.

"You were sleeping so soundly. I decided you must need the sleep. And it did you a lot of good too. I haven't seen you eat so much breakfast in ages."

Nickie quickly changed the subject. "How's Roger coming with the porch?" she asked.

"I'm afraid he isn't coming at all. Mrs. Miller phoned about an hour ago to see if he could come over and take a look at her power mower. It wouldn't start or something. And he's not back yet."

"I bet he has it all in pieces by now. She'll be lucky if he ever puts it together again."

"He'll get it together all right, but I don't know when that porch will get painted," replied her mother, and went back to her vacuuming.

Nickie rinsed out her glass and bowl, and filled her pockets with carrots. She looked around the pantry, but there wasn't anything else that looked like horse food. Finally she squeezed a few oatmeal cookies in with the carrots. After all, oats are for horses.

She found Gail and Corky in their grandmother's garage. Mrs. Walton did not have a car, but she was an avid gardener, and she used the garage to store her gardening supplies — spades and trowels, clippers and pruning shears, bags of peat moss and fertilizer, and a whole glittering row of things to spray with. Corky had his eye on these, and Gail had her eye on Corky. The kitten was there too, tangling himself up in a spool of green plastic plant ties.

"Well, you slept long enough," Gail greeted her.

"Nobody woke me up," explained Nickie.

"Lucky you. *I* was jumped on at seven-thirty by guess who. And I'm baby-sitting on him too because Dad's gone off to start work, and Mother and Grandmother have gone to look at houses. I haven't even had a chance to get up to you know where."

"Where?" asked Corky.

"Nowhere. Put those clippers down. They're sharp."

"Bring him over to our yard," suggested Nickie. "There's nothing he can hurt over there."

Corky made a beeline for Roger's old car and climbed up in the driver's seat, what there was of it. Right away he found the only thing that really worked — an old horn with a rubber bulb that Roger had fastened to the steering post.

The noise was terrible, but it kept Corky busy while the girls talked.

"Does that water faucet at the stables work?" asked Gail.

"No. Everything's turned off. But I had an idea. I could easily get an empty pail under the fence and through the tunnel. Then I could shove one end of the hose under the fence and pull it as far as it would go. It would reach from the faucet on the garage through the tunnel at least. I hope."

"Swell idea. And Grandmother's got miles of hose over there. She'd never miss a section if we borrowed it. I'll stay on this side and you give the hose a tug when you want the water turned on."

Quietly and quickly, Nickie got a pail from the basement, while Gail fastened two sections of hose together and put one end under the fence. She wedged a stone under the loose board to keep it from resting on the hose and cutting off the water.

All this time Corky was blissfully tooting away on the old horn. Nickie could still hear him as she crawled through the tunnel with the pail. Then she went back for the end of the hose. It slid through easily and reached well past the tunnel.

When she was ready, she tugged on the hose good and hard. After a couple of minutes water gushed from the end of it, and she filled the pail. Then she tugged on the hose again and it began to slither away like a green snake.

Nickie headed for the stables as fast as she could with the heavy pail. Water sloshed into her shoes, as she changed the pail from hand to hand. At the last big oak tree she set the pail down. She was almost afraid to go around the tree and look.

What if the horse wasn't there? What if there was nothing there except the same old row of empty stalls? What if it had all been a dream last night?

"Gail wouldn't have dreamed the same dream," she said out loud.

Instantly there was an answer to her voice. A soft welcoming whinny.

She picked up the pail again and hurried around the tree and across the stable yard.

There he stood. Her horse. Quickly she untied him and led him out to drink, talking to him all the time.

"I know I'm late and you're thirsty, but I won't be late again. There are so many things to figure out. But we'll get it down to a system, and then you'll really be in clover. I can't keep calling you

You, I'll have to think of a name. You must have had a name once. I wonder what it was? Never mind, you're going to have the best name in the world as soon as I can think of it. There, that was good, wasn't it?"

The horse drank in big drippy gulps, and knocked the pail over trying to get the last bit.

"We'll get you something bigger to drink out of," said Nickie. "Then we won't have to carry buckets all day. Here, have a carrot."

She fed him the carrots and the oatmeal cookies, and coaxed him back into his stall with the last cookie.

"You've had your dessert first," she said. "Now I have to figure out some way to get you some grass. It's a shame. Acres of grass out there that need cutting and you need the grass, but you can't go out and graze because somebody'd be sure to see you through the gates. Wait here."

Nickie ran up to the hayloft. The big old cushions had belonged to some wicker chairs her mother had thrown away, and the covers unsnapped and came off for washing. Nickie unsnapped two of them and shook the cushions out. The empty covers looked like old laundry bags.

Nickie made her way up to the lawn behind the house and tore off great handfuls of long green grass and stuffed it into the cushion covers. When they wouldn't hold a single blade more, she carried them, bumping and banging against her legs, back

to the stall and dumped them out into the manger.

Then she stood in the next stall, with her hands on the high wooden partition and her chin on her hands, and watched the horse eat. Her horse.

There was so much to do she could hardly decide where to start.

"Hi!" called a voice. Nickie nearly jumped out of her skin before she realized that it was Gail at the edge of the trees.

"Hi!" she called, running to meet her. "How did you get loose from Corky?"

"Mother and Grandmother came back."

"Did they find a house?"

"Not yet. Mother's still hoping to find one near Grandmother's, but she's beginning to get discouraged."

"Why, there are hundreds of houses around here."

"But not for rent, furnished. All the new ones are for sale, and the ones that are for rent are unfurnished."

"She'll find a place," said Nickie. "She only started looking yesterday."

"That's right. Yesterday was our first day here!" exclaimed Gail. "Gosh, it was a long day."

"It sure was," said Nickie, grinning. "It lasted all night."

Gail followed Nickie back to the stable, and looked the horse over thoughtfully.

"This is the first I've really seen him," she said.

"He has a really good head — or he did have, once. I wonder how old he is? He's big. If he ever got really filled out, he'd make two of Chip."

"Chip?"

"My horse at home. He's a cow pony, really, and his whole name is Chocolate Chip because he's mostly white with brownish splatters. Like chocolate chip ice cream, you know."

"I didn't know you had a horse," said Nickie.

"We all do," replied Gail.

"You didn't tell me," said Nickie.

"Well, you never asked."

"Corky too?"

"Butterscotch is supposed to be Corky's. She's a fat little pony, sort of tan, that used to be mine until my feet started dragging. Corky gets along fine as long as he lets Butterscotch do just what she wants. As soon as he gets an idea she doesn't like — bingo, she dumps him off. And then try and catch her!"

Nickie didn't say anything for a while. She had to get used to the idea that Gail had a horse. That everyone in her family had a horse. No wonder she was willing to waste a wish on curly hair!

Probably Gail thought that Nickie's horse, the horse she had worked so hard to get, was an old plug.

Wait a minute, Nickie reminded herself honestly. Gail worked hard to get this horse too. She was the one who opened the gate. What if she hadn't opened the gate? Nickie couldn't think of an answer; she couldn't even imagine an answer.

With an untidy bunch of long grass sticking out of his mouth, the horse rubbed his nose against Nickie's shoulder.

"He likes you," said Gail. "You know, he's very well-behaved considering where he came from and all. What are you going to name him?"

"I don't know," said Nickie. "Everything I think of is too fancy."

"You're right, he doesn't want a fancy name. He wants a good name, one that describes him."

"He's terribly tall," said Nickie. "Tall Boy? High Boy? Just one word — Highboy?"

"I like that," said Gail. "Yes, that's just right. Highboy. You know, a highboy's a piece of furniture too. My grandmother has one. And it sort of reminds me of this horse."

"A piece of furniture reminds you of this horse!" exclaimed Nickie indignantly.

"Yes, it does," insisted Gail. She frowned, thinking of a way to explain it. "It's a very tall chest of drawers. It's handsome, but it's useful too. And it's quite old, but it's worth taking good care of. My grandmother takes good care of hers. It's a wonderful sort of glowing brown, and polished like anything."

Nickie thought about what Gail said. It made her feel good about her horse.

"Highboy," she repeated. "That will be his

name. And he could be polished too, if we had the right brushes. Highboy, how do you like your new name?" Highboy moved his head gently up and down as Nickie rubbed his nose.

"There's so much to do, and so many things we ought to get," Nickie went on. "I keep thinking of more things. We ought to make a list."

"They'll be calling us for lunch any minute," said Gail. "And we sure don't want them sending Corky to look for us. Let's make the list after lunch. So long, Highboy, see you later."

Nickie gave Highboy a last pat. "We'll be back," she promised him.

As they walked away, Gail said, "And that highboy is another reason we ought to get out of Grandmother's house."

"Why?" asked Nickie.

"I can see Corky looking at it and thinking. He's thinking that he could pull each drawer out a different distance and climb up them. And then he would be clear up to the ceiling."

Porch Painters

"It took you a long time to fix that mower," Mrs. Baxter said as Roger rushed in for lunch, with black grease under his fingernails.

"It didn't take long to fix it," he explained, loading his plate with hash and salad. "I got it going all right, but there's still something funny with the gas feed. I can work it fine, but every time Mrs. Miller tries it she floods the motor. Catsup, please. So finally I just mowed the lawn for her."

"Well, good for Mrs. Miller," said Nickie. "Didn't Dad tell you to mow our lawn last week?"

"With our old hand mower? It takes a whole day at least. So how am I going to do that and paint the porch too?" asked Roger indignantly.

"Children, children," said Mrs. Baxter. "Roger, you really must get the rest of the first coat on that porch. If we have a hard rain, goodness knows when that new wood will dry out enough to paint."

"I know. I'll do it. But it's going to cost me real money. Honest, the way I figure it I can hardly afford to finish painting the porch."

"What are you talking about?" asked his mother.

"Mrs. Miller's power mower," explained Roger patiently. "She's had it in and out of the shop all spring, and it's been costing her plenty. She told me that if I would keep it in good running condition and keep her lawn mowed, I could use it myself the rest of the time. I know stacks of lawn jobs I could get. Why, I'd be rolling in money. I could buy a couple of little things I need for the car and have it running in no time."

"But you can't get a driver's license till next year," Nickie reminded him.

"And you can't possibly earn enough to pay a painter to put two coats of paint on that big porch," said his mother sternly. "That's your job for the summer. You agreed to do it."

"I know, I know," said Roger glumly. "I'll get on it after lunch. But I have to see some people first."

"What people?" asked his mother.

"Oh, I stopped at a few places on the way home and lined up some lawn jobs. Now I have to go back and tell them I can't do it."

"I'll paint the porch," said Nickie suddenly. "Gail and I will paint it and you can pay us out of your lawn money. We could use a little cash too."

"Would you?" asked Roger hopefully. "No kidding?"

"Sure. And we'll be twice as fast and we won't drip all over the place, either."

"Well, I just don't know," exclaimed Mrs. Baxter. "Could you girls really paint it properly?"

"You bet we could! Maybe we couldn't handle the big brush, but we could use smaller ones. They'd be better, anyway, for the railings. Fifty cents an hour for each of us — how about it, Roger?"

"It's a deal!" he shouted. "I can make three bucks an hour easy. Hop to it, kid. By the way, who won the Kentucky Derby in 1930?"

"Gallant Fox," snapped Nickie. "Who won the World Series in 1924?"

"Washington. Well, I'm off. Tell you what, I'll mow our lawn first — and free."

He pushed his chair back so hard it tipped over, and he rushed out the back door.

Mrs. Baxter set the chair upright again. "Nickie, you and Gail see what you can do with the porch this afternoon and we'll let Daddy have a look at it and see what he says. You know, I'm beginning to think this might be a very good idea."

"Sure it is," said Nickie. "Roger will work hard at anything to do with machinery. But stand around and paint? He'd just be a pain in the neck all summer, moaning and groaning."

Nickie's mother smiled at her. "You don't know how glad I am that Gail came to stay next door! You've been a different girl ever since. Daddy and I were beginning to think that we would have both of you moaning and groaning all summer."

"I didn't! Well, maybe I did. But no more moaning and groaning for me. I just haven't got the time."

Nickie found Gail and explained about the painting. "Just think of the things we can buy with the money. The only rush part of the job is the first coat. After that we can take our time. Besides, I like to paint. Of course, this deal is really between Roger and me. You don't have to paint if you don't want to."

"I helped paint a barn once," said Gail. "And it was six times as big as your porch. Let's get some paper and a pencil, and make out that list while we work. This is going to be fun."

By the time Nickie and Gail had started painting, Roger was back with the mower.

"Those mowers are handy things," said Nickie. "That apple tree sheds apples all summer. Every time Roger did the lawn with our old mower, I had to pick up all the apples first. But this thing just slices them into applesauce and keeps right on going."

The noise of the mower brought Corky on the run. For a few minutes he watched from his grandmother's yard, then he came over and fell in behind Roger, trotting along in the freshly mowed strip, around and around and around the lawn.

The kitten, however, was frightened by the racket. It shot up onto the porch and tried to crawl into Nickie's pocket to get away from it all.

"Smart kitty," said Nickie. "I'd hate to think what would happen to you if you got in front of that thing."

"You haven't even named that kitten yet," Gail reminded her.

"Poor kitty, I haven't paid much attention to you, have I? Never mind, you're a nice kitty and pretty soon I'm going to introduce you to a horse. How about Tigger for a name? Because he's stripy and bouncy."

"Tigger's fine. You know, Corky's just crazy about the kitten, and he's very good to it too. For Corky, that is. He strokes it, and it purrs like crazy."

"Maybe he thinks the purr is some kind of machinery inside," suggested Nickie.

The lawn was done in no time, and Nickie could see that Roger would indeed be rolling in money if his customers' lawns grew fast enough.

Roger cut off the motor and came over to inspect the painting job.

"Not bad, not bad," he said.

"Huh, listen to that," snorted Nickie. "We've already done more than you did all day yesterday."

"Are you all through already?" Corky asked Roger.

"All through here, Butch," said Roger. "Got a lot more places to go, though."

"Can I come with you?" asked Corky hopefully.

"Well — what would you do if you came?"

"Just watch," said Corky. "Just listen." He looked up at Roger with big, admiring eyes.

Roger scratched his head. "Would your mother mind?" he asked Gail.

"My mother positively would not mind one single bit," replied Gail. "And if you want to know, neither would I."

"Well — okay then, Butch."

"You behave now, Corky," said Gail. "And don't bother Roger. Understand?"

Corky just looked at her. He didn't say a word, but it was easy enough to tell what he was thinking. Bother Roger, who owned the beautiful car with the bouncy seat and the loud-honking horn! Bother the boy who ran the rackety grass-cutting machine! Sisters sure are peculiar.

"Well, keep up the good work," said Roger. "Come on, Butch. You and I got work to do."

They set off up the street — Roger pushing the mower and Corky, with one hand on the mower handle, trotting hard to keep up.

"Sometimes brothers are all right," said Nickie, looking after them.

She and Gail had set up an assembly line for

painting the railings. Nickie, using the stepladder, painted the outside of each upright rail and the side to her right. Gail, kneeling on the porch floor, painted the inside and the side to her right. That way, since they were both right-handed, they never had to poke the brush awkwardly to the left.

"Roger never would have thought of this in a million years," said Nickie.

"But it takes two people," said Gail.

"He wouldn't have thought of it if he was twins," retorted Nickie.

They stopped every so often to add more things to their list.

Real halter, if we can afford one.

Oats.

Currycomb.

Body brush.

Something big for water. Old-fashioned washtub?

Rope. Enough to crosstie for grooming.

Around the edges of the list, Nickie doodled little sketches of horses' heads. "What about bedding?" she asked. "That's a good clay floor in the stall, but oughtn't he to have straw?"

"Maybe. But straw's more important in cold weather. Put it at the bottom of the list."

"And a shovel for cleaning out the stall. I know," Nickie cried suddenly, "there's an old shovel nobody uses in our basement. It has a good square edge. I think it's left over from the time before we got the oil furnace, when there were coal and ashes to shovel."

"Have you looked at Highboy's feet?" asked Gail.

"He isn't shod, if that's what you mean. But on clay or dirt or grass — isn't that all right?"

"Sure," agreed Gail. "You won't be riding him on roads or rocky places. I wonder if he's ever been ridden?"

"He's pulled a wagon, or a plow, or something. He's got collar marks on his neck. Anyway, I won't even try riding him until he's fattened up a little. Imagine riding bareback on that backbone!"

"What I can't get over are his good manners," said Gail earnestly. "He's so used to being handled, and he leads so well. He's so gentle and — sensible. I think he was brought up with people. Now Chip was a range pony. Somebody roped him in a roundup and tamed him and broke him. But you can still tell that when he was a colt he was as wild as a coyote. Oh, he handles well and he can run all day and he can find his way home from anywhere — but there's a difference. I can't quite explain it."

"Even if Highboy's been pulling a wagon lately, maybe he was ridden when he was younger," said Nickie. "I guess I'll find out when I try it. He's so big — do you suppose he might have been a hunter? They hunt a lot down in Virginia, and that's quite near here."

"The thing about a horse is, you never know. He can't tell you."

"I read this book once," said Nickie eagerly. "About an old abandoned horse. It turned out that the horse was once a champion jumper at Madison Square Garden. But of course you know how it is in books," she added practically, "anything can happen. But I don't care. Even if Highboy never was anything wonderful or special, he's my horse."

When they finished the front railing, Gail suggested they take a rest. "I bet we've done two dollars' worth at least," she said.

"At least," agreed Nickie. "I'll collect from Mother and she can get it from Roger later. We'll go over to this old hardware store I know. They have everything — goldfish, kerosene lamps, mole traps, tulip bulbs, hay, feed, and grain. And if they don't have it, they're nice about getting it for you.... Say, I just thought of something! I have some money in my bank that I saved up. I was going to use it for extra spending money at camp. Boy, was I ever lucky those termites chewed up the old porch! And was I ever lucky I didn't go off to camp this year!"

Gail laughed so hard she had to sit down on the steps.

"What's so funny?" demanded Nickie.

"You!" spluttered Gail. "Lucky, lucky you!"

Money to Spend

The money, with sixty cents Gail found in her handbag, just stretched over a currycomb, a round, medium-sized galvanized-iron washtub, and five pounds of oats in a paper bag.

"It was a good thing one of those sacks had a hole in it," remarked Nickie. "Otherwise we'd have had to buy a hundred-pound sack. Not that we could have paid for a hundred-pound sack of oats in a hundred years."

"From now on, we'll only have the money we earn painting," said Gail. "What'll we buy next?"

"How about the brush," suggested Nickie. "Highboy doesn't really mind that old rope halter, and we ought to get to work on his coat — it's so ragged and dusty."

They had quite a time with the washtub. Gail finally had to hand it over the fence to Nickie, and Nickie had to roll it through the tunnel, which wasn't really big enough for it.

Nickie carried five pails of water to fill the tub, while Gail turned the hose on and off for her. Then Gail pulled the hose back into the yard. They both carried several loads of grass in the cushion covers.

"This is silly," said Gail. "Carrying grass to a horse. It would be much better for Highboy to graze. We can't really carry enough. He ought to graze for hours and hours to fill out those ribs."

"I know," said Nickie. "And another thing, we're wearing a terribly plain path up to the house. First thing tomorrow I'm going to pull the vines back across it, especially where it comes out behind the house. It's just an invitation for anybody to walk right down here. Then I'm going to make a new path."

"Where?" asked Gail.

"Starting at the bottom of the stable yard, over there, and right across to the side wall. Then along the wall to the front lawn. Nobody would ever notice it from the house unless they were looking for it. Then, if we get up early, we can take Highboy along that path and let him graze on the lawn for a couple of hours every morning before anybody else is awake."

"There isn't any such time in my house. Corky always wakes up first."

"I'll do it, then," said Nickie. "Maybe evenings,

too. Although it stays light awfully late this time of year."

"Some hay would be handy," suggested Gail. "I don't know if we could afford it, though. If we had a scythe, we could cut some of that tall grass and let it lie in the sun and cure."

"It would be a lot of work," said Nickie doubtfully. "And somebody might notice it was cut. Well, Highboy had a pretty good meal today — let's give him his oats for dessert."

She shook a small amount of oats into the bottom of the pail, and Highboy nearly knocked her down in his eagerness to get at it. He snorted and guzzled the oats down, and chased the last few grains around and around the bottom of the pail until not one was left.

"No more now," said Nickie, putting the rest of the oats high up on a beam, along with the currycomb. "We'll get to work on his coat tomorrow. I think maybe I'll paint some more after supper."

When they got back to the Baxters' yard, Roger and Corky were there, but they were much too busy to wonder where the girls had come from so suddenly.

Roger's legs were sticking out from under his car, and Corky was squatting on his heels, peering in under.

"Wrench," said Roger, in a muffled voice. "No, the other one. Right by your hand."

Corky handed the wrench in to him.

"Business booming?" inquired Nickie.

"Yup. Three jobs today. Two more lined up for tomorrow. Plenty more after that, if I walk a little farther to 'em. Then I'll pray for rain."

"Why rain?"

"Grass grows faster in wet weather. Hey, Butch, you wanna see something interesting? Stick your head under here a minute."

Corky crawled right in under the car, and they could hear Roger tapping on something and explaining it to Corky. Nickie and Gail hardly understood one single word, but Corky looked perfectly satisfied when he crawled out again with a smear of black grease in his hair and oil drips all down his back.

"Come in and wash up for supper," said Gail, but Corky didn't pay the slightest attention. "All right, then. Wait till Mother gets a look at you. Wait till Grandmother gets a look at you. . . . See you tomorrow, Nickie."

Mr. Baxter looked the front porch over when he got home, and came right in the house to congratulate Roger on doing such a good job for a change.

So there wasn't anything wrong with the way Nickie and Gail were painting. But when he found out the girls were painting the porch, Mr. Baxter decided that Roger must be putting something over on them.

Nickie had to point out that they really wanted

the job, and that Roger was paying them. Roger pointed out that he wasn't sitting around loafing. He was working very, very hard.

"And after I pay them for painting and buy just a couple of little things I need, I'm going to save up the rest. Why, the way I figure it, I can mow lawns all summer, every summer, and work my way through college. After I graduate from high school, of course."

"All right," said his father. "You've talked me into it. And that college you work your way through had better be a school of mechanical engineering."

After supper Nickie started in on the porch steps. She painted just halfway across, so people could walk on the unpainted side while the painted side dried. Just as she finished, Tigger, the kitten, came bouncing around the corner of the house.

Tigger was chasing a grasshopper. And he was catching it too. The grasshopper jumped; Tigger pounced and came down with his paw on the grasshopper; he looked to see what he had caught; the grasshopper jumped again, and Tigger pounced again.

Finally the grasshopper made a terrific leap and landed on the porch steps. Another leap, and it was on the porch. Tigger scrambled up the steps after it — on the painted side, smearing the wet paint. Then he ran around the porch, looking for his grasshopper and leaving painted paw prints on the unpainted boards.

"Tigger!" cried Nickie. "Look what you're doing! And just look at your paws!"

The grasshopper escaped through the railings, and Tigger sat down suddenly. He lifted one front paw and looked at it. He shook it, then licked it.

"Tastes awful, doesn't it?" said Nickie. "You'll get sick if you try to wash that paint off."

She carried the kitten into the house, upside down, with his little painted paws sticking up in the air.

"Oh, dear," said her mother when she saw the kitten. "I don't know what will take that off. Turpentine, of course, but that wouldn't be any better for him to lick off than paint."

"Oil will dissolve house paint," said Roger. "Salad oil. That's what I've been using to get the stuff off my hands."

"So that's what's been happening to my salad oil," said his mother. But she got the salad oil and helped Nickie clean the kitten's paws with it.

When they were through, Nickie sat down on the floor with the kitten on her lap. "Now lick your paws," she said. "Tastes better, doesn't it?"

Her father, behind the evening paper, said, "Looks as if they're finally going to widen Collier Drive, and about time too. That's a real bottleneck at rush hour."

"They've been talking about it for years," said Nickie's mother. "Nothing ever happens."

"I think it'll go through this time. Most of the big property owners that fought it so hard are dead now. All those big estates have been subdivided, except the Olds' place."

"I'll be surprised if Mr. Olds takes it lying down," commented Mrs. Baxter.

"So will I. Especially as it may mean that front wall of his will have to come down."

"Take down Mr. Olds' front wall!" exclaimed Nickie. "They can't do that!"

"They may just move it back twenty feet or so," said her father. "They're planning to put in storm sewers and sidewalks along there. He's always fought that too. And no wonder, as he'll be assessed to pay for part of it."

"Storm sewers! Sidewalks!" cried Nickie indignantly. "Who needs them?" One of the reasons the Olds' place was so private was because there was no sidewalk in front of it. Most people used the sidewalk on the other side of the street.

"They'll have to do it in time," explained her father. "It's much cheaper to tear everything up at once and get it over with."

"But when? When are they going to do all this?" asked Nickie anxiously.

"So far the highway commission has just set aside the money for it. First there will have to be hearings, and maybe appeals, and a great deal of surveying. Then they'll advertise for bids. I'll be very much surprised if they start work inside of a year and a half. Maybe even two years."

A year and a half. Two years. Nickie relaxed. Anything could happen in a year and a half, or two years.

"I almost feel sorry for the old man," said Mrs. Baxter. "Talk about King Canute trying to hold back the tide."

"Sorry for him?" exclaimed Mr. Baxter. "With all that money? Of course taxes must be taking a terrific bite out of it."

"Just the same, he must be pretty lonely since his wife died. Mrs. Walton used to be a friend of his wife's, but she never sees him any more. I gather he was always rather difficult to live with. His only daughter died as a child, and I don't believe he sees much of his son. After the son was married he and his wife lived in the place for a while with the old man, but it didn't work out. They live in California now."

The kitten licked and licked at his paws, and purred and purred. Nickie yawned and yawned. She was sleepy. And tired too.

She picked up Tigger and started upstairs with him. "Good night, everybody," she called down.

"Shall I put the kitten in the basement when I go to bed?" asked her mother. "Then you won't have to get up and do it — the way you did last night."

Last night. Was that only last night? It seemed a million years ago.

"All right," said Nickie. "Thanks."

"Good night, honey," called her father. "And thanks too. It just occurred to me that I have had two evening meals in a row without once hearing the word horse."

Hey, Hay!

The next day, Nickie did her best to blot out the path from the stables to the house. She straightened bushes and looped vines across them. At the upper end, near the house, she pushed a branch of poison ivy forward so that its dark shiny leaves were in plain sight.

Then she and Gail trampled out a fresh path across to the west wall and along the wall to the front lawn. Nickie was right; it didn't show at all unless you went clear over to the wall and looked for it. Even then it didn't look like much.

Soon Nickie was leading Highboy along the new path to graze in the early morning. She and Gail divided all their time between painting the porch and taking care of Highboy.

He was a very different looking horse now from

the one who had stood in the old shed with his head hanging down to his knees. It was hard to tell whether he was really filling out or whether he just looked better with his head up and a new gloss on his coat.

Nickie and Gail spent hours over him with the currycomb. At first the old dead hair had come out by the handful. As soon as they had earned enough money, they bought a really good body brush. They brushed him and brushed him until his dull coat began to shine.

"Lots of the horses out our way are pintos and calicos," said Gail. "I think an overall color like this is prettier. Now that we've polished him up, he's almost black. What color is he, anyway?"

"He's a brown, I think," said Nickie. "You don't see them very often. But the hairs on his muzzle are brown, and that's the way you tell."

"He sure enjoys being groomed," said Gail. "If he was a cat, he'd purr. Now, Chip just despises it — he acts exactly like Corky being sent back to wash his hands again."

But Highboy stood like a statue, except for twisting his neck around to watch. He took in everything with wise dark eyes and quick-moving ears. He even stood calmly while they sponged off his legs. When Nickie accidentally tapped him on the knee, he lifted his forefoot as if at a signal.

"Look at that!" exclaimed Gail. "He wouldn't raise a rumpus at being shod. You know some-

thing? This horse is remembering. You can see him remembering more things all the time."

"I know," said Nickie. "He's remembering back a long way — back to when somebody took care of him and loved him. And look, the collar marks on his neck don't show quite so much. I wonder if they'll ever go clear away?"

Because he stood so high, it was impossible for the girls to reach Highboy's back and mane. Nickie had dumped the books out of the orange crate in the hayloft and they used it as a stool. But that was awkward. So was sitting on the partition of the stall.

"I'm going to try getting up on him," she said to Gail one day. "Hold him, will you? I'm not sure what he'll think of it."

From the top of the partition, Nickie leaned forward and rested her arms across Highboy's back, lightly at first, and then more heavily. It did not seem to bother him at all, although, as usual, he looked around to see what was going on.

"I'd sure hate to have him crowd me against the wood and break my leg," she muttered. "How would I ever explain it to Mother?"

Finally, talking to him all the time, she scrambled from the partition onto his back, holding on around his neck. Highboy took a little step forward, as if to say, "Want to ride?"

Slowly, Gail led him out of the stall and Nickie straightened up, gripping lightly with her knees and holding onto his mane. Then Gail led him in a big, slow circle around the stable yard.

His walk was stiff and a little jolting, but it was not the slogging, shambling gait with which he had followed them from the animal shelter. He lifted his knees a little and even took a couple of quick prancing steps sidewise.

"How is it up there?" asked Gail.

"Wonderful. Just wonderful," breathed Nickie. "It's a little like riding the ridgepole of a barn, but I don't care. I'm riding him, and he likes it. He really does."

Gail took a turn while Nickie led. After that, whenever they wanted to brush Highboy's back or mane, they climbed up on him and went to work.

"If only we had a saddle and bridle!" exclaimed Nickie.

"A bridle, maybe, if your father would like a third coat of paint on the porch. But a saddle! Two hundred bucks! And remember, we have to keep on buying oats."

"Only one hundred ninety-eight dollars and ninety-five cents," said Nickie. They had looked it up in a catalogue at the hardware store. "Well, maybe a bridle and a saddle blanket. Some day."

Every day it was getting harder for the girls to find a time when they could pass the hose under the back fence without being seen. Roger, who mowed enough lawns to pay for the painting, was spending the rest of his time — and money — on his car. He tinkered around it and under it and in it, usually with Corky stuck to him like a shadow.

Nickie and Gail kept the hose connected to the faucet on the garage, and left it lying in careless loops near the fence, all ready to use whenever they got a chance. Roger and Corky rarely paid the slightest attention to them; still, it was awkward having them around so much of the time.

One day it was nearly noon before the girls managed to get up to the stables with fresh water. That was the day Roger started his car. He borrowed Nickie's bicycle pump and pumped up the tires, while Corky stood around and watched.

Roger finally put the pump away. Then he climbed in behind the wheel, warned everybody to stand back, and stepped on the starter. There was a loud bang, and a cloud of blue smoke drifted out from underneath the car.

Roger adjusted something and tried again. This time the motor caught with a whole series of bangs and settled down to a loud unsteady *putt-putt, putt, putt-putt-putt*! Everything on the car shook and rattled; more blue smoke billowed out and Mrs. Baxter came running out the back door.

"Listen to that!" bellowed Roger happily. "Just listen to that!"

"I am listening," shouted his mother, with her hands over her ears. "*Turn it off*!"

When the engine stopped, with a shudder and one last bang, Mrs. Baxter said, "I just want to make sure you don't have any ideas about driving that thing. Remember, no driving until you get your license."

"But just on the driveway," Roger protested. "Just on private property. That's legal. Besides, you ought to be grateful. This makes us a two-car family. Who knows, there might be an emergency some day, and then you'd be glad to get in this car and drive it some place."

"Never!" exclaimed his mother. "I'd rather roller skate."

So with Corky sitting beside him, Roger drove slowly up and down the driveway — forward to the edge of the street, backward to the garage, over and over and over and over again.

While this was going on, Nickie and Gail managed the hose and the water tub without a bit of trouble. By the time Gail had pulled the hose back into the yard, Roger had cut the motor off and was bending lovingly over the engine again, like a mother over a baby.

When Gail got up to the stables, she heard the motor start up again. "Sounds different," she said. "Sounds better."

Nickie listened, frowning. "It is different," she said. "It's coming from the other direction. Listen."

They listened. It *was* coming from the other direction. Quickly they ran along the path by the wall to the edge of the underbrush and looked out.

The front gates were wide open, pulled clear back against the wall. Way down near the gates a big mowing machine was clattering along by the wall. The driver, under a yellow umbrella, was sitting high up on a little jouncing seat, and the long cutting blade was laying the tall grass down in a wide swath.

"I told you they mowed it every so often," said Nickie. "This is the first time this year. That caretaker must have come and unlocked the gate. I sure hope everybody goes away again when the grass is cut," she added uneasily.

Gail pulled her back along the path, close to the wall, and shouted, "Hay!"

"Hey what?" asked Nickie, startled.

"Hay! Just *hay*!" cried Gail. "Acres of hay! Tons of hay! Just look at it all! We'll give it a while to lie in the sun and dry, and then we'll rake it up and carry it to the stables."

Of course. Free hay, for the carrying. The best hay in the world — lawn grass run wild, with tall patches of red clover and hardly any weeds at all. Nickie did a little dance, and Gail joined in.

"I've been worrying about next winter," said Gail. "Grass and oats are fine, for now, but here it is July already, and the porch is nearly done, except for the very last coat on part of the ceiling, and some years hay is just terribly expensive. It depends on the weather and the grass crop and all."

The noise of the mowing machine got louder, and they went back to the end of the path and peered cautiously out. The machine was up near the house now, cutting around the rhododendrons and the jutting porches with a good deal of backing and maneuvering. Then it clattered around the other side of the house where they could no longer see it.

"Good thing I covered up that path," muttered Nickie. "Still, that man has his hands full, with that big cutter and the gears and all."

They listened intently. The man seemed to be spending a great deal of time cutting the stretch of grass between the back of the house and the edge of the thicket.

"What if he takes a notion to slice a path through to the stables?" whispered Gail anxiously. "He almost could, with that thing."

"Nobody ever has," replied Nickie firmly, but she felt much better when the machine swung back into sight around the far corner of the house.

It wheeled around and cut back and forth a couple of more times in front of the house, straightening out the path it had cut around the porches and bushes.

"See, he's cutting himself one big oblong," said Nickie. "Then he can just go around and around, right across the driveway, every time."

She and Gail backed down the path and hid in the bushes as the mower chugged across the upper edge of the lawn on their side. It left a neat, square edge, toppling tall grass, seedlings, and honeysuckle tangles. At the corner, it backed and turned and clattered off down the lawn beside the wall.

Now there was just one huge oblong lawn, several acres of it, to cut around and around. Nickie and Gail watched for a few minutes longer and then went back to the stables.

"Hay, Highboy! Hay!" exclaimed Nickie, throwing her arms around the big horse's neck. "We'll pile it up to the ceiling, and you can stand around all winter and get fat as a pig. Still, I'll feel better when that man goes away and we have the place to ourselves again."

"You said no one ever bothered to come down to the stables," Gail reminded her.

"I know," replied Nickie uneasily. "I don't *think* anyone ever did. Naturally, we always made ourselves scarce when there were people around the house. But I don't know for sure that nobody ever came down and looked around because if they did, there wasn't anything for them to see unless they climbed up the ladder to the hayloft. All I know for sure is that nothing was ever touched or changed around here. But how would you hide a horse, if you had to?"

"Couldn't we put Highboy in the carriage house?" asked Gail.

"It's only got half a door. The other half's been off for ages. It's on the ground, over that way, all grown over with brambles and the wood is rotting off the hinges."

"What about the room behind the stalls?"

"That's an idea. Let's look."

It was a dark, narrow room that ran the length of the stalls. Even with the door open, it was dim and eerie inside. There was one small dirty window high up at the far end. An electric wire with an empty socket dangled from the middle of the ceiling, and there were cobwebs everywhere, and trash all over the floor.

"We never cleaned up in here," explained Nickie. "It's a horrid place. I wonder what they used it for?"

"They probably kept the tack for the riding horses in here," said Gail, poking around in the littered corners. The harness and stuff for the carriage horses was probably kept in the carriage house. You sure they didn't leave any old bridles or saddles around?"

"Just trash and rats' nests and cobwebs," said Nickie. "I suppose we could lead Highboy in here in a hurry if we ever had to. And I sure hope we don't ever have to! Gee, I wish that man would finish the lawn and go away. I'm starved, but we ought to stick around and keep an eye on things."

"I know," said Gail. "Look, you run home and grab something to eat. When you get back, I'll go."

"Okay," said Nickie. "I'll hurry."

No Way Out

When Nickie got home, her mother said, "You're late. We've already had lunch, and Roger's gone off on a lawn job."

"That's all right," said Nickie. "I'll just grab a sandwich."

While she was piling jelly and peanut butter on some bread, she had an idea. She made two huge sandwiches, put them in a paper bag, and stuck in a handful of plums and half a box of cookies. Then she took the whole thing next door.

When Gail's mother came to the door, Nickie asked, "May Gail and I have a picnic lunch outdoors today? I've got one already packed."

"That's a fine idea," said Gail's mother.

Corky pressed his nose against the screen door and asked, "Where are you having a picnic?"

"Oh, just a place," replied Nickie. "I have to run. Gail's waiting for me."

"Where?" Corky called after her. "Where is she waiting for you?" Nickie pretended not to hear.

She could feel Corky staring after her, so she went the long way around. She went across her own backyard, past Roger's car, and down the driveway on the far side of the house. Then she cut across into the Harringtons' yard. The Harringtons were away for the summer. Nickie walked clear to their back fence before she slipped through the hedge into her own yard, behind the garage.

Fine thing, Corky on their trail. He'd never shown the slighest interest before in what they did or where they went. She'd have to remember to warn Gail.

At the stables, she spoke to Highboy and fed him one of the cookies. Then she went up the path looking for Gail.

Gail was lying on her stomach at the end of the path. "The mowing machine finished up and a man came and paid the driver and he went away," she reported breathlessly. "But the man that paid him is still here, and look — something else has just come!"

Nickie looked. The front gates were still open and there was a truck parked just inside them. Two men in overalls were talking to another man, not in overalls.

"That's the caretaker, I think," said Nickie shading her eyes and squinting. "Yes, that's his car out on the street. Oh, I almost forgot. Food!"

"Hot diggity. I'm *starved,*" Gail exclaimed. They ate by touch, groping around in the lunch bag for their food, never taking their eyes off the men and the truck. The caretaker stood around with his hands in his pockets while the two men in overalls worked around the gateposts with hammers and chisels.

"I know what they're doing," said Nickie suddenly. "They're mending the rusted hinges. Boy, are we ever lucky we got those gates open when we did! When you did, I mean."

"Tell me," said Gail, licking the last of the plum juice from her fingers. "This wall around the property — does it go all the way back on both sides?"

"Yes," said Nickie. "Clear to the back corners of the place. It's a block across the front — a long block — and two and a half blocks down each side. The houses and yards on our street go across the back of it."

"Do all the people on your block have back fences?"

"Sure," said Nickie. "There's a chain-link fence at the back of your grandmother's and at the back of the house next door to her, which is the last house at that end," she explained. "Then there's our fence, and the Harringtons, next door, have one of those split-sapling jobs, about seven feet high. They have a double lot, so there's just the Martins left, and brother, is that a fence! They have a Doberman and he bit the mailman once. So the police told them to keep that dog fenced in. Their whole backyard's fenced with high wire, and barbed wire on top."

The men down at the gate were putting their tools back in the truck. It had taken both of them, with the caretaker lending a hand, to lift the heavy gate and set the hinges into the new iron rings on the gatepost. They swung the gate back and forth a couple of times, and closed both sides to check the fit in the middle.

Then the caretaker opened both sides wide, and the men got into their truck and drove away.

Nickie heaved a big sigh of relief.

"Now if the caretaker will just kindly scram," she said. As if in answer, the caretaker closed the gates, put the padlock through the center bars, and snapped it shut. Then he pulled on it to make sure it was locked.

"*Now* what is he doing?" asked Gail. "Why doesn't he just go away."

"Oh, I know," said Nickie. "The signs. He's putting them back on the gate."

"KEEP OUT. PRIVATE PROPERTY. TRESPASSERS WILL BE PROSECUTED," recited Gail and Nickie together.

"Now he's getting into his car," said Nickie. "And there he goes, at last! *Wheee*!"

They ran back down to the stables and hugged and petted and talked to Highboy to make up for leaving him alone so long.

"What a wasted day!" exclaimed Nickie. "Lurking around and watching. Of course we got something out of it. Six or seven acres of hay."

"And a good thing too," said Gail. "I suppose you know what that mended gate means."

"No. What?"

"It means we're locked in. At least Highboy's locked in. He's inside a stone wall and an iron gate and a row of fences. There's no way out."

It was several days before Nickie and Gail felt really safe again at the stables — and alone. They spent long hours feeding and grooming Highboy, and taking turns riding him around the stable yard. But it was hard to keep their minds on what they were doing.

They talked in voices lower than usual, and sometimes, in the middle of a sentence, they would break off to listen.

They kept hearing things. Usually it was only a squirrel, dropping green acorns on the carriage-house roof. Sometimes it was the distant rattle and chuff of Roger's car. But even though they knew it was Roger's car, they would hurry up the path, to make absolutely sure it wasn't something driving in through the front gates.

And even when they didn't hear anything at all,

but when it was too quiet for too long, they would tie Highboy and take a long, careful look around.

The rows of windows on the tall house still glittered emptily and the doors were shut and locked. The big iron gates were shut and locked and on the lawn the mowed grass was turning yellow, and fresh new grass was beginning to poke up through it, like a green carpet.

Finally Nickie discovered a great truth. "You absolutely cannot keep on worrying forever about anything," she announced one day. "Even if it is something you need to worry about. Worrying sort of wears itself out."

Besides, they had something new to worry about. With the porch all painted and paid for, and the car actually making noises and moving, Roger up and quit mowing lawns.

"What about that college you were working your way through?" inquired Nickie.

"For Pete's sake, I've still got two more years of high school left!" he protested. "What do you want me to do — turn into an infant prodigy?"

"Fat chance," replied Nickie scornfully.

So there was Roger, practically all day, every day, right in the backyard. And where Roger was, there Corky was too. And where Corky was, there Tigger was.

Tigger grew enormously and became fierce and adventurous. He quit tagging around at Corky's heels, begging to be picked up and petted. He discovered his claws and looked around for things to climb. The cherry tree bark was too slick. The apple tree was fine, until Tigger bounced too hard on a branch and brought down a shower of green apples, like hailstones, all over himself.

Tigger began climbing the pear tree. And the pear tree stood by the back corner of the garage, and overlooked the loose board in the fence.

Tigger could get up the pear tree just fine. But as soon as he even thought about getting down, he opened his mouth and screeched for help. And it was usually Corky who scrambled up and plucked Tigger down.

Once Tigger even climbed up the fence and balanced, wobbling, on the top. Corky was running to rescue him when Nickie beat him to it.

"And suppose Corky tries to climb up on the fence himself!" Nickie said to Gail. "And what if he fell off!"

"He's tough," said Gail. "He'd bounce."

"It's not that!" exclaimed Nickie. "What if he fell off on the other side? He'd land right smack in the tunnel — and then what? Why can't he go in the house and find something to do?"

Gail grinned. "You sound just exactly like my grandmother," she said. "Only she says, 'Why can't he go *outdoors* and find something to do?' "

Falls Church

Next morning Roger went off to see a friend who was also working on an old car and Corky, for a wonder, was nowhere in sight. Nickie waited impatiently for Gail to come and help with the faucet and hose.

Suddenly she heard sobs and wails coming from Mrs. Walton's house. The sobs changed to roars of rage and there was the sound of somebody kicking something, hard.

Then Gail came out the back door and jumped over the hedge.

"What in the world — " asked Nickie.

"Corky, throwing a tantrum," explained Gail briefly. "Let's hurry with the water while we have the chance."

After Nickie had filled the tub, Gail pulled the

hose back into the yard and went up to the stables.

"What ails Corky?" asked Nickie, leading Highboy over to the tub.

Gail didn't answer right away. She ran her hands over Highboy's ribs as he drank. "He's really fattening up," she said. "It's not just the shine on the outside." Finally she answered Nickie's question. "Corky's having a fit about something Mother said."

Gail looked so unhappy that Nickie didn't ask any more questions. After all, families are families and they have a right to a little privacy.

After Highboy had drunk he tried to get his nose into Nickie's pockets, where she often carried carrots or cookies for him.

"Not this morning," said Nickie, gently pushing his head away. "Stop it, you big clown. Honestly, you get sillier every day."

"Stronger too," said Gail, as Highboy nickered and tried to see if there was anything in *her* pockets. "You know something? If he goes on feeling better and better, we aren't going to be able to control him with just that old halter. The only reason we could do it before was because he was half dead. We absolutely are going to have to get a bridle and bit for him some way."

"You're right," said Nickie. "Anyway, it's a good thing there are two of us."

Gail didn't say anything for a minute. Then she said, not looking at Nickie, "Corky was roaring because he said he wasn't going to live in a church and have to wash his face and wear his Sunday-school clothes every day."

"Whoever heard of anybody living in a church?" asked Nickie. "What got into him?"

"It was something Mother said. She said, 'We are going to live in Falls Church.' "

"Falls Church!" repeated Nickie. "She didn't mean it, did she?"

Gail nodded.

"But, Gail, *Falls Church*! You can't go and live *there*! Why, it's in Virginia. It's across the river. It's miles and miles and *miles* from here!"

"I know," said Gail. "Mother and Dad told us all about it. Then Corky threw another fit and said he wasn't going, he was going to stay here and live with Roger. That's what he was yelling about when I left."

"But — but — but — " stammered Nickie. "I thought your folks were looking for a house near *here*. They want to be near your grandmother. They said so."

"They do. So does she. But they've looked and looked, and absolutely the only place they could find was in Falls Church. They say they were lucky to find it. It's exactly what they were looking for — plenty of bedrooms, a big yard, three blocks to a school, furnished just right, which means good enough but not so good we have to watch Corky all the time. It sounds like a perfectly wonderful place," she ended miserably, "and I just hate it already."

"Oh, Gail!" wailed Nickie. "You can't go! What will I do without you? What will Highboy do without you? And I've written Joan and Mollie all about you, and about how now there will be five of us, which is a much better number than four. And I wrote Debby too. She thinks she's so great because her uncle's letting her drive a racing sulky with some safe, old, broken-down trotting horse. I told her you had a real cow pony. I've been saving Highboy for a surprise when they all get back. Oh, I wish you could stay here and live with me. Why couldn't you?"

"Because I couldn't, you know that."

"No, I don't. Listen, Gail, I've got it all figured out!" cried Nickie eagerly. "You wouldn't even have to use the spare room. My room is good and big, and the other half of my bed, the top part of the double-decker, is up in the attic. All we have to do is get it down. And my closet is huge. There's plenty of room for all your stuff too, and we'd be in the same room at school, and we can take care of Highboy together! How about it?"

"Oh, Nickie, you sound just like Corky," said Gail, almost smiling. "People can't just go off and leave their families, even if they don't like where they're moving to. I hate to go, like anything, but just the same I'll go. I can come and visit you, and you can come and visit me."

"No, I can't," said Nickie sadly. "You'll be so far away you can't ever come unless your mother drives you, and then she'll have to bring Corky along too, and nothing will be fun anymore."

"I feel just as bad about it as you do," said Gail. "Worse, because you're home, and your friends will all be back pretty soon, and you'll have plenty to do whether I'm here or not. Look, I have four more days and I'm not going to spoil them by sitting around in a puddle of gloom the whole time. Let's get the hay in. It's good and dry, and we've been lucky it hasn't been rained on yet."

"Oh, Gail, you're so sensible!" wailed Nickie. "All right, we'll get the hay in. But where'll we put it? It really belongs in the hayloft, but we can't get it up there — unless we carry it in our teeth. We need our hands to climb the ladder."

"Oh, Nickie," Gail laughed. "The floor of the carriage house will do. It's a perfectly good place for hay."

They had already figured out how they would move the hay. They had brought a couple of wide bamboo rakes from home, which nobody was likely to miss until it was time to rake leaves in the fall, and two of Nickie's old camp blankets. They spread the blankets on the ground and raked the hay onto them. Then they dragged the blankets to the end of the path and tied the corners together, like sheets full of laundry. They hauled these big bundles, bumping and scraping, down the path to the carriage house and shook the hay out on the floor.

All the hay that was properly dried they piled up along the walls. Any that was still a little green, they spread out on the floor to finish drying.

They worked hard all day, and still there was at least six times as much hay left on the lawn as they had raked up, and the carriage house smelled wonderful.

"Mmmm," breathed Nickie, with her nose burried in an armful of hay. "Grass dried in the sun. Nothing else smells half as good. I wonder if it tastes the way it smells?"

"Well, don't eat it," said Gail. "It's for Highboy. And by the time we get it all in, there really will be enough to get him through the winter."

Even though the hay was for next winter, they heaped Highboy's manger with some very choice clovery samples, just to see how he was going to like it.

"Look at him go for it!" exclaimed Gail. "Gee, I'm going to miss everything here. I'm going to miss Highboy. And I still miss Chip."

"Who's taking care of him while you're away?" asked Nickie.

"The people who rented our house. They're nice and they know about horses — but it isn't the same. And I know Mother misses Tennessee Girl.

She's Mother's very own, a Tennessee walker, and such a lady. Nobody but Mother was ever allowed to ride her. Until now, of course."

"Does your father ride a lot too?"

"Well, he's pretty busy. He spends a lot of time in some of the wildest places, looking over mining properties and things like that. Mostly he uses a jeep, but sometimes a mule. He says a mule can get places that nothing else can, not even a helicopter."

"Does Corky miss his pony?"

"It's hard to tell with Corky. Sometimes I think he'd trade Butterscotch for Roger's old car, and throw in the saddle and bridle and the barn too!"

At supper, Nickie broke the sad news to her family. Her mother had already heard it from Gail's mother, and she felt almost as bad as Nickie did.

"It's a shame," she agreed. "You and Gail have been together so much. I'd really like to do something special for her before she leaves. I don't know about a party, with all the other girls away and all. Has she seen any of the sights in Washington yet? We could take the boat down to Mt. Vernon one day. Or go to the zoo. Or the Smithsonian, or the Monument, and then have lunch at the National Gallery. Do you think Gail would enjoy something like that?"

Nickie thought about it. "Why don't we wait until Mollie and Joan and Debby get back, and then invite Gail to a real super-duper party? She only has four more days left, and I really think she'd like us to go right on doing what we have been doing."

"Oh dear, I do wish her folks had been able to find a place in the neighborhood," said Mrs. Baxter regretfully. "You and Gail have kept each other so busy. I just don't know what you'll do after she's gone."

Nickie almost said, "I'll be kept even busier." But she didn't.

Mr. Olds

All the next day, and the next, Nickie and Gail hauled hay.

They piled it up around the walls of the carriage house as high as they could reach. It was hot, hard work, and they got hay in their hair and down their necks and in their socks and shoes. But they got about half the hay safely under cover.

The following morning, when Nickie reached the stables with the first pail of water, she stopped and stared.

There was a big puddle of water under the old iron faucet; its damp edges spread halfway across the stable yard. Nickie dropped the pail, and turned and hurried back down the path and through the tunnel.

"Psst! Gail!" she called softly, tapping on the fence. "Come quick. People!"

"Who? Where?" asked Gail, as she caught up with Nickie.

"I don't know," said Nickie breathlessly. "But look! The water's on here." She turned the faucet off hard, and the dribble stopped. "So somebody's turned it on up at the house. We better go look. Come on."

"Let's get some good out of the water first," said Gail practically. "It might go off again any minute."

Hastily they shoved the tub under the faucet and filled it up, clear to the brim. But they didn't lead Highboy out to drink; they just piled his manger with hay to keep him busy and quiet and ran up the path to the edge of the lawn.

The big front gates were wide open. From the end of the path they could see only the front of the house, sidewise, and at first they didn't notice anything. Then Nickie whispered, "Look. Windows open. Upstairs, front corner."

"Can't we get closer?" asked Gail anxiously.

"Sure. Come on."

Nickie dashed back down the path and then began working her way directly up toward the back of the house through the tangled underbrush. Gail followed.

For the last few feet they lay down and squirmed along, where curtains of honeysuckle draped over the bushes and left a little clear space near the ground. Finally they reached a spot where they could lie flat and look out through a thin screen of stems and leaves, and could see and not be seen.

The caretaker's car was parked by the back door, and beside it was a large truck with lettering on the side of it:

COMPLETE CLEANING SERVICE
Homes, Offices, Apartments
Call us for free estimate

The kitchen door was wide open. Men in coveralls were washing the downstairs windows. The upstairs windows had already been washed; you could tell by the shine. Nickie and Gail had never seen anybody clean windows so fast. Through the clean windows they could see other men in coveralls moving about, and they could hear the dim hum of a vacuum cleaner.

"Electricity's on too," whispered Gail.

The caretaker walked out the back door and across the drive and the back lawn. Then he turned and stood with his hands in his pockets, inspecting the back of the house. He was so close to the girls that they could have reached out and touched his shoes. They hardly breathed until he walked back to the house again.

It was hot and prickly under the honeysuckle vines. Swarms of tiny biting gnats hummed around their ears and got caught in their hair and eyelashes, but they didn't dare scratch or brush them away. The ground they were lying on was full of roots and small stones. And still they lay there.

Watching. And listening. And worrying.

At last the men in coveralls came out the back door carrying their cleaning equipment, and began stowing it in the truck. They went in and out, shouting back and forth to each other, so that there seemed to be dozens of them. When they were all settled in the truck, however, there were only six. Then the caretaker came out of the house with a check in his hand. He handed the check to the driver of the truck, who put it in his pocket, started the engine, and drove off.

The caretaker went back into the house and disappeared from sight.

Nickie and Gail waited. And watched. But nothing happened.

At last Gail whispered urgently, "These gnats are killing me. Let's get out of here for a bit."

They wiggled backward until it was safe to stand up, and then picked their way back to the stables. Gail ran straight to Highboy's water tub, dipped her hands in, and sloshed water all over her face and head.

"Whew! That's better. Listen, what's going on up there? Have they ever done this before? Run around washing windows, and all?"

Nickie plunged her whole head into the tub and came up streaming. She tossed her hair back and answered, "Well, they have had the windows washed before."

"Well, I don't like it," said Gail fiercely. "It

looks as if they're getting ready for that old man — what's his name — to come and stay."

"In *July*?" exclaimed Nickie. "He wouldn't come to Washington in July. August either. You can see for yourself what the weather's like."

"Didn't he ever come in July?" persisted Gail. "Not ever?"

Nickie thought. "No. He comes in the spring and fall. He has places in Palm Beach and Bar Harbor, Maine, and he comes here in between."

"But, then what's this all for?" demanded Gail. "I don't like it."

"Me either," admitted Nickie. "But that caretaker has done things around the house before, and then just locked up and gone away."

"Well, then, let's hope he just locks up and goes away now," said Gail grimly. "The sooner the better."

"Maybe he already has," said Nickie hopefully. "Let's go back and look."

They went back the same way. Even before they reached the edge of the bushes, they could hear noises. Kitchen noises.

The caretaker's car was still parked by the back door. Through the open kitchen windows they could see someone moving around, clattering pots and pans and opening and closing drawers.

"Car coming," whispered Gail. "Listen."

A delivery truck rattled around the corner of the house, scattering gravel, and pulled up with a squeal of brakes. The driver hauled out a big carton of groceries and knocked on the back door.

"*Capitol Market!*" he bawled.

A cross-looking woman in a dark uniform with a white cap and apron came to the door. "In here," she said.

The driver dashed in, and out again, and carried a second big carton of groceries inside. Then he jumped back in the truck. Instead of following the drive on around the house, he backed and turned, crashing the rear of the truck into the bushes, not ten feet from where Nickie and Gail were lying, and roared off the way he had come.

"He could kill somebody like that," muttered Gail. "Two cartons of groceries, and somebody to cook 'em. That's bad."

"It's not good," admitted Nickie.

They watched the cook, or whoever she was, moving around, putting the groceries away, then go off somewhere, out of sight.

Again they waited. And waited. Gnats zinged around their ears and sweat trickled down the backs of their necks. Finally they went back down to the stables.

"What are we going to do?" demanded Nickie.

"What is there to do?" replied Gail. "Just wait and see."

"That's the hardest thing there is to do," said Nickie crossly. "Waiting and seeing."

They led Highboy out to drink, then tied him up

again and gave him some more hay. Every so often they tried the water faucet again, just to see if the water was still on. They knew it would be, and it was.

And every so often, both of them, both at once, without a word to each other, hurried silently up the path by the wall for another look. The gates were still open. The upstairs windows were still open. That was all.

Once Nickie whispered, "Highboy's not locked in any more. If they leave the gates open all night, we could get him out."

"And take him where?" asked Gail.

"Nowhere," said Nickie. "That's just it."

Back at the stables, Nickie filled the pail with water and set it inside the tack room. Then she carried several armloads of hay in and piled them in a corner.

"What's the good of that?" demanded Gail. "Nobody's going to find Highboy unless they come right down here. And if they do, they're going to see the hay in the carriage house and the footprints in the mud where the faucet leaked. Then they'll *really* look. And there he'll be."

"I know," said Nickie. "But it's something to do."

They went back up the path again. This time there was something to see.

A black car was coming slowly up the driveway. It was an old car, long and high, and the headlights grew out of the front fenders on stalks, like snails' eyes.

"That's it," muttered Nickie. "Same old car. He's had it forever."

The car stopped in front of the steps and a uniformed chauffeur jumped out and opened the rear door. The passenger stepped out.

It was Mr. Olds, all right. He straightened up slowly, a tall, thin old man, dressed all in black and white — white suit, black necktie, and shoes. In one hand he carried a Panama hat, in the other, a cane. He walked stiffly up the steps, a white-haired old man with heavy black eyebrows. It was hard to tell whether he was frowning fiercely or whether the eyebrows just grew in a fierce frown. As he crossed the porch, he slashed at one of the pillars with his cane. It was an angry gesture.

Gail let out a long breath. "I knew all along he would look just exactly like that," she whispered.

The caretaker came out of the house and helped the chauffeur lift suitcases down from a sort of railed platform on top of the car — two big suitcases and one perfectly enormous one.

After a few minutes the caretaker drove off in his car, but the big shiny black car stayed right where it was, in front of the house.

So now, inside the house were Mr. Olds, a chauffeur, and a cook. Not to mention three suitcases and two cartons of groceries.

Nickie and Gail went slowly back to the stables.

"Well, now we know," said Nickie. "It's funny, but I almost feel better. I mean, I'm still worrying, but I'd rather know what I'm worrying about than wonder what I'm worrying about."

"Me too," said Gail. "And, jeepers, all of a sudden I'm starving to death. I wasn't a bit hungry before. Look, if I go for food, I'm likely to get stuck with Corky. You go. I'll stay and watch."

Nickie's mother met her at the back door. "Is Corky with you and Gail?" she asked.

"No, we haven't seen him all morning. I'm going to fix us something to eat. How about the leftover fried chicken? Can I take some?"

"Of course. Perhaps he's with Roger. I saw him myself about an hour ago, playing with the kitten, but nobody's seen either of them since."

Just as Nickie was hurrying out with the lunch, Roger strolled in.

"Have you seen Corky this morning?" asked his mother.

"Butch? Nope. Been over at Johnny's. He's working on this old Plymouth, and it's a beaut. He needs to buy a few little things, and I was thinking about lending him Mrs. Miller's power mower — "

"Oh, dear, perhaps he's turned up at home by now," said Mrs. Baxter anxiously. "Run over and ask, will you, Nickie?"

Nickie took the bag of lunch and went next door. "Gail and I are having a picnic lunch," she said to Gail's mother. "Has Corky turned up? He wasn't with us, or with Roger."

"Oh, that wretched child. He's been threatening to run away and hide until we leave. Then he plans to move in with Roger. I'm not really worried — he'll come home when he gets hungry. Wait — take some cinnamon buns for your lunch. I bought a dozen yesterday."

Nickie waited anxiously while Gail's mother searched the kitchen and pantry. Finally she said ruefully, "Perhaps Master Corcoran won't get hungry as soon as I thought he would. I'm afraid that if you and Gail want cinnamon buns for lunch, you'll have to find Corky first. If you do, send him home, will you?"

"We'll look for him," promised Nickie. "And we'll send him home, all right, all right."

She turned slowly away. Where would Corky go if he wanted to hide out? She was afraid she knew the answer.

When she got out to the back fence, she was sure she knew the answer. Abandoned on the piece of two-by-four board that ran across the fence near the top, was part of a cinnamon bun — the part around the edge, with the least sugar and cinnamon on it.

Nickie boosted herself up and looked over. Corky's tracks were clear enough: a squashed clump of ragweed at the bottom of the fence, where he had jumped down, and a trail of stepped-on vines and weeds that led away from the tunnel and the path to the stables. If Corky had gone in that direction, no wonder they hadn't seen or heard him.

So, Corky, with eleven cinnamon buns and perhaps Tigger, was loose inside the grounds of the Olds' place. They absolutely had to find him and get him out of there fast. Why, he might do *anything.*

Nickie decided against following his trail. If he didn't want to be caught, all he had to do was sit quietly in a thickly overgrown spot, and she would never in the world find him unless she stepped on him.

Nickie went under the fence and hurried up to the stables to find Gail.

A Horse in the Stable

Gail wasn't at the stables. Before Nickie went any farther, she looked carefully around on the ground. It was still impossible to cross the stable yard without walking where the faucet had leaked. The damp ground was covered with footprints — hers, Gail's, Highboy's. But nowhere was there a print of a very small shoe. Or the round, tidy print of a kitten's paw.

So far, at least, it looked as if Corky hadn't found the stables.

Gail was up at the end of the path, waiting impatiently for the lunch.

"Seen Corky anywhere around?" asked Nickie, dealing out cold fried chicken.

"Corky? I should hope not!"

"Well, I'm afraid he's in here." Between bites, Nickie explained. "And this side of our back fence is just smooth boards, no toeholds, so he can't get out of here again except by the front gate."

"He hasn't gone out the gate," said Gail positively. "I've had my eye on it the whole time. Mr. Olds had a visitor, but he didn't stay long. Fellow with a briefcase."

"A lawyer, I bet," said Nickie. "I just remembered something, and I bet it's the reason he's here at such a funny time of year. They're going to widen Collier Drive and put in sidewalks and storm sewers. Dad said Mr. Olds would get mad and try to stop it. But look — what are we going to do about Corky? Mr. Olds is absolutely fierce about trespassers. If he ever caught sight of Corky, he'd take off after him — or have the chauffeur do it. And it would be just our luck to have Corky go crashing down to the stables, or to our path, with somebody right after him."

"Yes, but we can't very well run around shouting for him," Gail pointed out. "Besides, if he's running away, he wouldn't answer if we did."

"I think the main thing is to keep him away from the house, if we possibly can," said Nickie. "If you watch from the bushes here, where you can see this whole side of the house, I'll go around on the other side and do the same thing. Then whoever finds him can try to get him back to our fence, without using the tunnel, and boost him over."

"Okay," said Gail. "And I sure hope he catches it when he gets home."

"I know one thing he'll catch," said Nickie grimly. "Poison ivy. He crashed right through the biggest patch of it down by the fence!"

Nickie went down the path to the stables, and from there struck out for the far side of the house. There were several big tangles of wild blackberries she had to work her way around, and near one of them she came across Corky's trail. A patch of honeysuckle had been well flattened, as if it had been sat on for some time, and right in the middle of it was another half-eaten cinnamon bun.

She couldn't be certain in which direction he had gone from there. He must have been traveling close to the ground, perhaps on his hands and knees. Nickie kept on going, stopping often to listen for noises. She thought she saw a little movement in the bushes off to one side. Then she was sure she did.

"Corky," she said softly.

"Meow," came the answer, and Tigger bounced out and rubbed around her ankles. There were bits of dried leaves stuck in his fur and spiderwebs on his whiskers.

"Where's Corky?" asked Nickie. But Tigger wasn't interested. He sat down to rub the spiderwebs off his whiskers.

"Oh, Tigger, I guess I'd better put *you* in a safe place."

She backtracked with the kitten in her arms and shut him in the tack room. Tigger didn't resist. He had done enough running away for one day. He curled up in the pile of hay and went right to sleep.

Nickie worked her way back around the house until she was near the edge of the bushes on the far side. Then she sat down to watch and listen. But there was nothing to see and nothing to hear.

It was midafternoon, hot and sticky; nothing was stirring, not even a breeze. No birds would sing until evening. Even the squirrels, which were usually so busy in the big oak trees, were quiet and out of sight. Nickie was sure that if Corky moved in the bushes anywhere near her, she would hear him.

Everything was so breathlessly still that she could hear the cars swooshing by on Collier Drive.

Perhaps Corky was close by, as quiet as she was, waiting for her to go away. Maybe, if he thought she had seen him, he would move and give himself away. She spoke in a soft, coaxing voice, just above a whisper. "Corky. Hi, Corky. If you eat all those buns, you'll get a stomachache. How about one for me?"

There was no answer, no rustling among the bushes.

Then the front door of the house closed with a sharp click, and Nickie wormed her way to the very edge of the bushes and looked out.

Mr. Olds was on the front porch, walking back and forth, back and forth. It reminded Nickie of the tiger at the zoo.

The old man came down the steps and walked along the front of the house toward Nickie. Every so often he stopped and looked at the straggly rhododendrons and switched at them with his cane. At the corner of the house, he turned and walked back the other way, still switching at the bushes.

Nickie thought, why can't he go inside and find something to do? Then she almost giggled, because it was exactly what she had so often thought about Corky.

At the far end of the house he turned again and started back. Suddenly he whirled around and stood looking, with his back to Nickie. She straightened up until her head was above the bushes, trying to see what he was staring at.

Across the full width of the front lawn, in the afternoon shadow of the west wall, something was moving; something was coming along the path from the stables.

It was Corky! Where was Gail? What was she doing all this time? And why did Corky have to pick the one time when Mr. Olds could see him?

It was not only Corky, it was Highboy too! Corky, holding the rope, was leading Highboy out from the shelter of the path, out from the shadow of the wall. There they stood, in shocking plain sight, on the sunny lawn.

In the hot silence, Corky's high voice carried clearly. "Come on, horse. Here's plenty of grass. Go ahead, eat."

With an angry swish of his cane, Mr. Olds started toward the little boy and the big horse. Nickie tore herself loose from the vines and raced across the lawn. She overtook Mr. Olds and kept right on going. Ahead of her, Gail pulled one of her pigtails loose from a bramble branch, crashed out of the bushes, and reached Corky first.

She shouted at him and Corky answered calmly, "He's mine. I found him when I was looking for Tigger."

Highboy was startled by the commotion and the angry voices. Nickie took the rope from Corky and led the horse a few feet away and spoke to him quietly.

Then Mr. Olds was right beside them, speaking rapidly in a harsh voice.

"What is this? What is all this? Trespassing on my property. Didn't you see the signs?"

With the gates opened outward, the signs were out of sight, but Nickie and Gail knew what they said. PRIVATE PROPERTY. KEEP OUT. TRESPASSERS WILL BE PROSECUTED.

"Well? Well? You did see them. Didn't they mean anything to you?"

"No," said Corky. "I can't read."

"Invading private property, and with a horse too. Fine state of affairs. Now get out, all of you."

Nickie started blindly toward the gate, leading Highboy. Gail got a good grip on Corky and followed.

"Stop!" called Mr. Olds.

They stopped.

"Which one of you is the owner of this horse?"

"I am," replied Nickie in a muffled voice.

"He's a disgrace. A scarecrow. You should be ashamed of yourself, letting him get into this shape. No idea how to treat a horse. Fine state of affairs."

Nickie turned back to face the old man. "Don't call my horse a scarecrow!" she shouted furiously. "He is not a scarecrow. If you think he's a scarecrow now, you ought to have seen him when we got him! His ribs stuck out that far and he couldn't even hold his head up. We do know how to treat a horse, and we've been treating him just right, and he hasn't done your stables one bit of harm!"

"What? What?" spluttered Mr. Olds. "My stables? What's this about my stables?"

"We've been keeping Highboy in your stables," said Nickie distinctly. "There wasn't any place else to keep him, and the stables were just going to waste. They could fall down flat for all you care. We're not ashamed of ourselves. We're proud. We rescued him from being put out of his misery because he was old and thin. And now we have to take him away, and there isn't any place to take him to, and everything we did is wasted."

Nickie burst into tears. Corky took one look at her and began to cry too.

"Stop crying," exclaimed Mr. Olds irritably.

"Stop it! I can't stand people sniveling. You, girl," he pointed at Gail, "is this true?"

"Yes," said Gail. "All of it's true."

"Well, well." Mr. Olds slashed at the grass with his cane. "Fine state of affairs. Then where do you think you are going with this animal?"

"Back to the animal shelter, I guess," replied Gail. "They'll kill him. And that will make you a murderer."

The old man's black eyebrows drew together in a ferocious scowl, but when he spoke his voice was not angry. "Call me names, hey? Couple of vixens, I see. Both of you. Make free with my stables, hey? Haven't been near 'em in years. Let's see how much damage you've done. Come along."

Nickie had stopped crying. "We haven't done any damage," she said. "So we don't have to go back there."

Mr. Olds just stood aside and pointed with his cane. "Lead the way," he ordered. "Since you know it so well."

Gail went first, then Corky, then Nickie with Highboy. Mr. Olds brought up the rear. Down the path beside the wall, across to the stables.

Mr. Olds walked slowly around the stable yard, looking at everything — the water tub under the faucet; Highboy's clean stall, with hay in the manger; the shovel in the corner of the next stall; and the currycomb and brush and small paper bag on the ledge.

"What's in that?" he asked.

"Oats," said Nickie.

Suddenly there was a plaintive meow from the depths of the tack room.

"Tigger!" shouted Corky. "I hear him. Where is he?"

Nickie opened the door and Tigger shot out. Corky scooped him up.

"Something else of yours?" inquired Mr. Olds.

"Yes," said Nickie. "We rescued him too."

Mr. Olds looked into the carriage house at the hay stacked by the wall and spread out on the floor.

"Where did that come from?" he asked.

"Your front yard," replied Gail. "It was just going to waste."

"You two vixens brought that all the way down here? All of it? All by yourselves?"

They nodded.

"Might be a fire hazard. Ever think of that?"

"Not any more than it would be up in the hay-loft," said Gail. "There was hay in the hayloft once, wasn't there?"

"Hay in the hayloft? Certainly. Carriages in the carriage house. Horses in the stalls. Matched bays, ride or drive. A spotted pony for a little girl with pigtails like yours. Eyes like yours too."

He pulled an enormous gold watch out of his pocket and snapped the lid open.

"Teatime," he said. "Put up your horse."

"What?" asked Nickie.

"Put him up. In the stall. Tie him, and come with me, the lot of you."

"Where?" asked Gail suspiciously.

"Up to the house!" roared Mr. Olds. "Don't you understand plain English? I'm inviting you to tea."

People in the House

Mr. Olds turned abruptly from the carriage house door as though he expected to walk straight up the old drive to the house. The wall of vines and bushes brought him up short. He flicked a trailing vine with the tip of his cane and turned back.

"Back the way we came, hey?" he commented. "You go first. Have to be led around my own property. Fine state of affairs."

Nickie and Gail went first. Mr. Olds followed them, and Corky trailed along far to the rear. It wasn't until they reached the front porch that Gail noticed that Corky was carrying both Tigger and a rumpled dirty bag of cinnamon buns.

"Where did you get that?" whispered Gail. "You can't bring it in the house."

"I can too," Corky whispered back fiercely.

Gail gave up. Mr. Olds was holding the heavy front door open to them, and they walked past him slowly, hesitantly, into the house.

The hall was dark and wonderfully cool. A carpeted stairway stretched up and up, almost out of sight at the top. The only furniture in the hall was a strange thing with carvings around a diamond-shaped mirror and brass arms to hang hats and coats on.

Mr. Olds stepped over to one side and opened up a doorway by pushing a sliding door that disappeared silently into the wall.

He led them through it into an enormous, dim, cool room. Everything in it was dark, except a marble fireplace at one end that looked too clean and cold to have ever had a fire in it. Heavy pieces of furniture were lined up along the walls, and all the blinds were drawn to within a foot of the sills.

Nickie and Gail and Corky stood huddled together in the empty middle of the dark room. Mr. Olds went over to a window and raised the blind. It flew out of his hand and snapped clear up to the ceiling, letting a long shaft of afternoon sunlight in across the carpet and up the opposite wall.

Corky stared up at the blind with his mouth open. "How are you going to get it down again?" he asked with interest.

Without answering, Mr. Olds walked across to an enormous sofa and ran his foot over the carpet in front of it, feeling for something. He stepped down hard, and somewhere in the back of the house a buzzer sounded.

The cross looking cook appeared in the doorway. She stared at the three children as if she could not believe her own eyes.

"Tea," ordered Mr. Olds. He counted heads. "Tea for four."

"Yes, sir. In here?"

"Certainly in here. As soon as possible."

Corky said to nobody in particular, "I'm not allowed to drink tea."

"Milk, then," said Mr. Olds. "Have we any?"

"Yes, sir," replied the cook.

"Chocolate milk?" inquired Corky hopefully, but she was already gone.

"Well, well. Sit down, shall we? Anywhere, anywhere."

Nickie, Gail, and Corky sat down on the big sofa, close together, right in the middle of it. Corky set his paper bag down beside him and held Tigger tightly in both arms. His feet were stuck straight out in front of him. Nickie's and Gail's feet dangled uncomfortably, inches off the floor.

Mr. Olds pulled a big armchair away from the wall, shoving it around until it faced the sofa. Then he too sat down.

"Everybody all right, hey?"

They nodded silently.

"Good. Now, about this horse. Your parents know you've been keeping a horse in my stable?"

Nickie and Gail shook their heads.

"Did it all on your own, hey? Been a good horse in his day too. How did you say you got hold of him?"

Nickie looked at Gail. Gail looked at Nickie.

"We didn't say," replied Nickie politely.

"So you didn't. Had him long?"

"I don't remember exactly how long," replied Gail.

"You don't remember. Well, what did you plan to do with him? Remember that, hey?"

They looked at him without speaking.

"Cat got your tongues, hey? You talked fast enough just now. Had plenty to say for yourselves."

Nickie cleared her throat and said, "We don't want to talk about him anymore. It wouldn't do any good."

"It would only make us feel worse," said Gail. "The same as if he was dead."

Corky said suddenly, as if he were repeating something he had been told, "You don't talk about dead animals at a party. It's not polite."

The cook appeared in the doorway just then with a heavy silver tray of tea things, and Mr. Olds fetched over a low table to set it on. There were three thin china cups for tea, a pitcher for cream, and bowls for sugar and lemon. There was a tall glass of milk for Corky, and a flat silver plate with thin, thin slices of bread and butter.

Corky was still holding Tigger in his arms.

"Just a moment, please," said Mr. Olds to the cook. She came back to the tea table. "Take this kitten out to the kitchen. See what it will have. A saucer of milk, perhaps."

The cook's eyebrows flew up until they nearly reached the white cap on her head, but she reached out, took Tigger, and carried him off.

Corky took an enormous swallow of milk and wiped his white milk moustache off with a heavy linen napkin. He looked doubtfully at the bread and butter, then opened the bag of cinnamon buns and shook them out on the table.

"Have some," he said generously. "Oops, ants. Not very many, though."

"*Corky!*" said Gail under her breath.

The flicker of a real smile swept across Mr. Olds' thin face. "Thank you, my boy," he said graciously. He picked up a crushed cinnamon bun, shook a couple of ants off, and bit into it. "I can remember when bread and butter for tea seemed like cheating."

While Nickie and Gail waited for the scalding tea to cool, Corky took alternate bites of cinnamon bun and gulps of milk. He beamed at everybody. "A real party," he said happily. "Fun, huh?"

Nickie and Gail took small sips of hot tea. Mr. Olds passed them the plate of bread and butter.

"No thank you," said Gail.

"No thank you," said Nickie. "I'm not hungry."

She wasn't hungry. She wasn't thirsty, either. She set down the teacup. She wasn't anything. She just wanted to go off, away from everybody.

"Thank you for the tea," she said politely. "We have to go now."

"Thank you for the tea," said Gail. "And don't worry, we'll take our horse when we go. You can keep the things we bought. We won't be needing them."

"I'll get Tigger," cried Corky, dashing off in the direction of the kitchen.

Nickie and Gail stood up.

"*Sit down!*" thundered Mr. Olds. He scowled at them. "Who told you you could go? Who told you to take your horse away?"

Gail scowled right back at him. "You did!" she said. "You said, '*Get out*,' "

"Sit down," repeated Mr. Olds in a pleasanter voice. "Please," he added. It sounded as if he hadn't said "please" and really meant it in a long time.

"That's better. Now. Haven't had a chance to talk. Can't get an answer to a civil question. Fine state of affairs. What if I said, 'Leave your horse here?' What if I said, 'No harm done, here's a key to the front gate, come and go as you please'? What then, hey?"

A wild hope leaped up inside Nickie. But she was afraid to hope. She answered carefully, "It would depend — if you really meant it."

"Meant it? Of course I meant it!" snapped Mr. Olds. "Keep your horse, you vixens. Room in the stable. Grass on the lawn. Keep it cropped, save money for mowing."

"Really?" cried Gail. "Honestly?"

"Really?" gasped Nickie. "Really and truly?"

"Really and truly and honestly," Mr. Olds replied.

They couldn't sit still. They leaped off the sofa with a whoop and did a dance in the middle of the rug. Corky came in with Tigger, and Gail swung him off the floor and whirled him around and around with his feet flying through the air.

"Quit it!" gasped Corky.

"Meeeow!" protested Tigger.

Gail let them down and grabbed Nickie by the wrists. They swung around and around in circles. Nickie's short curls stood on end, and Gail's long yellow pigtails flew out like swing ropes.

Corky got his breath back, thanked Mr. Olds for tea, and started for the door. "I'm going home," he said.

"Wait, Corky, wait!" cried Nickie. "You can't get out the back way. You'll have to use the front gate. Can you find your way home from there?"

"Sure," said Corky, and departed, carrying Tigger.

Nickie and Gail stood still at last, with pink cheeks and shining eyes and ruffled hair.

"We didn't even thank you!" cried Gail.

"Thank you, *thank* you," said Nickie solemnly. "I guess you aren't used to people acting like this," she added apologetically.

"A little girl used to live here," said the old man. "Acted exactly like that. Sometimes. Regular vixen."

"Oh, was she the one that had the spotted pony?" asked Gail. "I'd like to know her. But she must be grown up by now."

"No. She died."

"Oh, I'm sorry," said Nickie.

"So am I," replied Mr. Olds. "But it was a long time ago. Sit down. Both of you. Tell me about this horse."

They sat down and told him, both talking at once. They told him about the night they stole Highboy — rescued him, really — and the trouble they had with the front gate, and how they happened to name him Highboy. They described the loose board in the back fence and the secret path up to the stable and how they managed about water with the hose and bucket. They told him about the porch they had painted and exactly what they had bought with the money.

"And maybe he does look the least little bit like a scarecrow," admitted Nickie honestly. "But he looks pretty good to us, because we know what he looked like before."

"And he's getting stronger and smarter every day," said Gail. "And now that he can go out on the lawn and graze all day, every day, in plain sight — why, the first thing you know, there won't be any holding him!"

"About that bucket brigade," suggested Mr. Olds, "I'll see what can be done about water down there. Even when it's off at the house. Must be some way, what?"

"That would be wonderful," said Nickie. "But we can manage if we have to."

"Get a vet in to look him over, hey?" went on Mr. Olds. "Have a look at his teeth. Let you know if he wants shoeing."

"Well —" said Gail. "We're all out of porches to paint, and I don't know about paying a vet — "

"And if we did have the money," said Nickie, "we'd much rather get a saddle, if we could."

"Saddle, hey? Must be some around somewhere. Cleaned out the stables when we bought a motor-car and gave up the carriage. Stored everything. Look it up for you, hey?"

"Oh, would you? *Could* you? Oh!" cried Nickie. "Now we can really ride Highboy!"

"Good. Share the rides evenly, hey? No squabbling over whose turn," said Mr. Olds.

Gail's face fell. "I forgot," she said sadly. "Everything's happened so fast, I forgot. I won't be here. We have to move to Falls Church day after tomorrow."

"What's that?" Mr. Olds looked really disturbed. "Move to Falls Church? Why?"

"Well, you see, Nickie's the one who lives here. It's her back fence we came through. I'm just visiting my grandmother next door, and now my mother and father have found a house to rent in Falls Church," explained Gail.

"Nonsense. Let 'em find a house near here."

"But they can't," said Gail. "There just aren't any for rent, furnished, around here.

"They looked and looked," explained Nickie for her. "Naturally, they wanted to live near Mrs. Walton — Gail's grandmother."

"Mrs. Walton? Not *Abby* Walton? Your grandmother?"

Gail nodded. "I'm named for her."

"Abby Walton's granddaughter. Bless my soul. Great friend of my wife's — Abby Walton. They were in school together."

Mr. Olds put his finger tips together and scowled at them. Then he looked at Gail from under his heavy black eyebrows and asked suddenly, "How would you like to live here? Hey?"

"Here!" exclaimed Gail, looking around at the huge room.

"Why not. My lawyers keep after me about taxes. Sell the place, they say, or get some revenue out of it. Subdivide, they say. Subdivide over my dead body, I tell 'em. . . . They will too," he added grimly. "But not until then."

"I — I'd love to live here," said Gail. "I'd love it more than anything."

"Tell your father to come and see me," said Mr. Olds. "Any time tomorrow. Fix it all up, lease and everything. Charge him whatever he was going to pay for the other place. I must run now. Appointment. Going to make a little trouble for the highway commission." He stood up. "Won't do any good," he said, chuckling. "But it'll give 'em something to think about. Good-bye."

They stood up and shook hands.

"Thank you, oh, thank you," said Nickie.

"I'll tell my father," said Gail. "And thank you again."

Not Secret, Not Stolen

Nickie and Gail walked slowly out the front door, and slowly down the front steps. Everything was different from the way it had been when they walked up the steps and in the door.

They looked down at the iron gates, and they were beautiful gates. They could go in or out any time they pleased, and it didn't matter who saw them. They walked across the lawn to the path by the wall. Just as they got there, Mr. Olds and the chauffeur came out of the house and went down the steps to the car.

Nickie and Gail waved, and Mr. Olds raised his cane in salute. He got into the car, and it moved slowly down the driveway; it was a beautiful car.

They went down the path to the stables and looked around. Everything looked different here too.

Nickie drew in a deep breath. "I know it's all true," she said. "But I don't *believe* it yet."

"I know," said Gail. "I'd better go home now and talk to Mother and Dad. I hope Dad's home."

"But will they want to live here?" asked Nickie anxiously. "Will they, really?"

"Yes, I think so," said Gail. "They even talked about it once, when they were looking for a house. They said, 'What a shame, that big house going to waste,' and they asked a real-estate man if he had ever talked to Mr. Olds about renting it. The real-estate man said yes, he had, and Mr. Olds had practically thrown him down the front steps."

Nickie grinned. "I bet he did too. But what about the other house? The one in Falls Church. Did your folks sign a lease, do you know?"

"It won't matter. There were six or eight people after that house, and somebody else will be glad to take it."

"Then you *will* be living here! I'm almost beginning to believe it."

"Me too. And I guess you'd better go home and talk to your mother too," said Gail.

"What about? We aren't moving."

"What *about*!" exclaimed Gail. "Listen, Highboy won't be a secret anymore. How can he be, with us living here and you taking him out on the lawn and riding him all around? And your father and mother don't even know you've got a horse! Or had you forgotten that?"

Nickie blinked. "I'd forgotten," she admitted. "But what if they want me to take him back? I won't take him back. I won't do it."

"Why should they?" asked Gail reasonably. "They said you couldn't have a horse because you didn't have any place to keep a horse, and you *didn't* have any place to keep a horse. At least, not any place you could tell them about. But now you do. You have a swell place and Mr. Olds *wants* you to keep Highboy there. It's perfectly simple."

"Is it?" asked Nickie. "Maybe it is. Sure it is. But I don't know what they'll say about the way I got Highboy."

"They'll say it's fine," said Gail stoutly. "Especially when they see him."

"I know," cried Nickie excitedly. "I'll just go back to the animal shelter and tell the truth. Tell them I have Highboy, and a wonderful stable for him, and over two acres to keep him on. We can sign the papers and he'll be really adopted — like Tigger."

"That's right," said Gail. "Not stolen. Adopted."

"Not secret, not stolen!" cried Nickie. She threw her arms around Highboy's neck and gave him a big hug.

"Do you hear that? You're not secret, not stolen anymore. Let's celebrate."

Nickie got the pail from the tack room and dumped the water out. Then she recklessly poured

in all the oats from the paper bag and propped the pail up in the manger.

"And, boy, am I glad of it," she went on. "Secrets are fun and terribly exciting, but after a while they sort of wear you down. Let's go home and tell everybody everything."

They hurried down the path to the tunnel.

"Another thing," said Gail. "We won't have to go this way anymore. We can walk right in through the gates."

"But that's such a long way around. This is a swell shortcut. Why don't we take that board right out of the fence, maybe take out two boards, or three, and make a real gate. We can turn the tunnel into a path. No more crawling," said Nickie, as they dropped on their hands and knees and began to crawl.

"But what about the other girls?" asked Gail anxiously. "Debby and Mollie and Joan? It's their tunnel too, isn't it? And their secret place in the hayloft?"

"Sure, but they'd much rather have Highboy to ride and help take care of, I know they would. And listen, when they all get back, I bet we could clear out the drive from the stables up to the house. All of us, working together."

"You bet we could!"

They pried up the board and crawled under.

Corky and Tigger were safely home. They were sitting in the driver's seat of Roger's car and

Roger's legs were sticking out from underneath.

"After we move in, my father might let Roger keep his car there," said Gail thoughtfully. "Around back, maybe, where it wouldn't show. I just hate to think of that long driveway going to waste."

"Swell. You know something? Every single thing at the Olds' place was just going to waste, and now we'll be using all of it."

"Remember when we picked the cherries for pies?" asked Gail. "And you said if you had just one wish, you'd wish for a horse? Now you've got your wish."

"Sure I remember," said Nickie. "And remember what you wished for?"

"Sure. It's what I always wish for."

"Well, maybe it's the humidity here that people are always complaining about but — "

"What are you talking about?" asked Gail.

"Your hair. It's starting to curl. Just a little and just around the edges, but it really is."

"It isn't! Is it?" Gail's hands flew up to her head. She ran her fingers across her forehead where wisps of loose hair had escaped from her braids. The wisps were curling in little damp tendrils.

"*It is*!" she cried. "It really is! Now I believe everything! See you later."

Gail ran across the yard, jumped over the hedge, and ran into the house next door, shouting,

"Mother! Mother!"

Nickie watched her go. Then she started for her own house, slowly at first, and then faster and faster. She ran up the back steps and across the back porch. She pulled the screen door open.

"Mother!" she shouted. "*Mother*!"